MARA JANE

THE GAME OF LOVE

part 1

Troubador Publishing Ltd
Unit E2 Airfield Business Park,
Harrison Road, Market Harborough,
Leicestershire. LE16 7UL
Tel: 0116 2792299
Email: books@troubador.co.uk
Web: www.troubador.co.uk

ISBN 978 1805142 652

British Library Cataloguing in Publication Data.
A catalogue record for this book is available from the British Library.

Printed and bound in Great Britain by 4edge Limited

To all the women in this world,
who never thought it would
happen to them...until it did!

Chapter 1

Jordan was sitting at the bar talking to the girl behind it.

"Slow night, isn't it?" she said.

"It's all right" said Willow, "It's a Tuesday!"

"...and it is still too early..." Gaby, her friend, added "have a drink and relax."

'Scores' is one of the most popular gentlemen clubs, not only in NY, but in the entire USA. Jordan had been working here for a week. It was last month when she flew in town looking for a job. She liked the Club. Easy money, very quick easy money! She'd met a few girls, made a few friends and her world changed. Only yesterday, she'd checked out of her hotel and moved in with Frank, into his two bedroom apartment, just across the street from the Club. It was a beautiful place, brand new, with spectacular views over the Queensboro bridge. She still couldn't believe how lucky she was to move there. Frank was a successful businessman from California and was in NY for only a few days a month, so, more or less, she was going to have the place all to herself.

"Do you want another Cosmo?" Willow said and dragged Jordan out of her thoughts.

"Yep, thanks love", she looked around and couldn't see Gaby. She was gone, probably to the showroom, looking for someone to get all the cash out of his pocket

Gaby was from Puerto Rico, living in Miami. She'd been working in 'Scores' for a year now. Once a month she'll fly down to NY and stay for a week. 23 years old and incredibly good at what she does! A born teaser, she was nicknamed Jessica Rabbit for her looks, smiley face, long red hair, big fake boobs, small waist, and sexy round butt. Just irresistible.

"Did you see where Gaby went?" Jordan asked, but no one gave her an answer.

It was midnight. The club normally closed at 4 in the morning, but Jordan didn't want to stay 'til the end. She had come early today and had gotten lucky. She'd made more than 1500$ already and was getting bored, sitting at the bar, getting tipsy. Unfortunately, she couldn't see her other friend, Paris, who always had some charlie on her. Drugs and strippers, two things that went together like butt and underwear. Paris was from Scotland, but she'd been dancing all around the world for a long time. She'd made dancing her profession and was going to retire from stripping one day......but where was she tonight? "I guess the back room," Jordan thought.

Paris was always in the private rooms. Jordan knew she was giving cocaine to the guys and that's how she kept them busy in there for most of the night. Once they got high, they lost track of time. It cost them five hundred dollars per hour "… crazy world…" she thought and smiled to herself.

"Hey Jordan, are you free?" it was Gaby again, "I got this guy up there in the Champagne VIP lounge. He is drunk and wired, but he spends lots of money."

She was pulling Jordan from the bar through the showroom to the VIP lounge.

"You got to talk to him because I am sitting with someone else. Last time he was here, he gave me round 3000$…he does party a lot, but so do you…so you will be fine."

They entered the Showroom and Jordan looked around, surprised. She hadn't realized there were so many people in there, because it had been so quiet on the other side by the bar. There were more than two hundred men in there. All the girls were busy dancing, or talking, or just flirting. The music was loud and the air smoky. 'Scores' was the only night club in NY, where you could have a cigarette. Nowhere else. It was impossible to be a smoker in that city anymore!!!

"Here" Gaby took her hand and pulled her through the crowd. "Oh my God I had no idea it was so busy" Jordan mumbled…

"Don't worry about that, down on the floor, they don't have any cash. Buying a few dances. Losers!! Come hurry up, before someone else has taken my guy away" and they rushed towards the champagne lounge.

There were no tables there either. Bottles of Crystal everywhere.

"Hey Jordan, where have you been babe, I was looking for you?"

"Hi Justin, I'll be right back with you honey. Got to say hello to somebody, don't go anywhere". She gave him a hug and a quick kiss on the cheek, "Don't move Justin and behave yourself." "I'll be waiting right here" he winked.

"Jordan, where were you?" another one called from the corner

"I've missed you, come say hello."

"I can't babe, I will later, ok?…"

"Oh my God I'm so popular tonight for some reason" she thought to herself and smiled.

Everybody loved Jordan, and why wouldn't they?!!

Even though she'd only been here for a week, she'd met most of the regular guys who came to the club. Jordan was always smiling, open and sociable and she liked to talk. She was an entertainer after all. That's exactly what it said on her work application: 'an entertainer', not a dancer!!

"Babe, can I introduce you to my friend?" said Gaby, smiling seductively, looking at the guy sitting in front of her. He looked up puzzled.

"Jordan, Nicholas… Nick is a sweet guy, aren't you Hun? Well, I will leave you alone for now, but we'll catch up later. Must check up on my friend over there."

She blew Nick a kiss and pushed Jordan to him. Jordan didn't say anything at first, just looked down at the man sitting in front of her. God, was he drunk?! What should she say to him? He hadn't even registered her presence, his eyes were still fixed on Gaby's sexy butt.

"What was your name darling?" Jordan asked.

He looked at her and froze. She was stunning! He couldn't remember ever seeing a woman prettier than her… or was that the alcohol messing with his head?…and what was a woman like that doing in a strip club?

Jordan was standing there looking at him waiting for an answer and he couldn't say a single word. Oh yes, she was beautiful. Her long blond hair was straight and silky, falling over her naked shoulders. Her eyes were dark and shiny… staring at him… wow!

"What was your name, love?" She asked again and smiled, showing her perfect white teeth.

Jordan was 5´8 tall and around 125 pounds, put together in an incredibly fine, and at the same time, very sexy package. Her legs were longer than most of the models Nick had seen in NY. Her breasts were just right, not too big, but not too small either. All natural and wrapped in flawless skin.

Nick was lost. The girl standing in front of him was breathtaking. She barely had on any makeup, which was a most unusual thing for a place like this. Her big brown eyes were looking straight into his, with a wondering, surprised look in them, as if she were asking herself, "What's wrong with this man?" He just wanted to touch her, make sure she was real. Before he could do anything, she turned around and walked away. She was so graceful, it was almost unreal.

What was that woman doing here and where did she come from? What was her name again? All these questions were bouncing in his mind. He had to do something. He had to find her again, talk to her.

The best thing to do would be to find Gaby, she would have all the answers.

Jordan had found her friend again sitting in the corner, talking to an older gentleman, who was pouring her a glass of champagne.

"I am sorry to interrupt," Jordan said addressing him, "but I need to talk to this sexy young lady for a second."

She turned then to Gaby, without even giving him a chance to protest or give her an answer.

"Listen babe, I am going to go back to the bar. It's almost 12.30. That guy is so wasted, I really can't be bothered talking to him… he can't even talk. He's so drunk, he doesn't even know his name. Ha. I'll have one more drink to switch off and after that, I'll be gone." She gave Gaby a wink, smiled and walked away…

"… oh my God, I forgot about Justin," Jordan thought and made her way to the opposite corner of the room, where Justin was sitting with his friends.

One hour later, she was still sitting with the boys. Justin was not just a client, he was also her friend. A bad influence though! Not even five minutes after she'd joined the table, he'd offered her a 'bomb' and had slid the small white package into her hand, without any of the security guys being able to notice a thing. Jordan didn't hesitate even for a second. She loved cocaine. It made her feel so excited anytime she had a line. She was going to feel miserable the day after, but that's tomorrow and now was now. And now she was flying. She was high up in the sky. She couldn't stop talking, and everyone was listening to the funny stories she was telling.

"That's what I call a 'one woman show'" she said, after looking around and noticing that she was entertaining the whole crowd all by herself again!!

"What's up Justin, shall we kill a shot? Last one and then I am leaving! Tequila?!"

She laughed and waved to the waiter.

"Thank God I don't need to walk far, ha, since I live across the street I can just roll over there. You'll walk me home, Jussy?" The waiter put two Kamikaze shots in front of them.

"To you" Justin said, and they both emptied their glasses in one gulp.

"Ok, let's move. I am going to get myself changed and I'll see you outside."

She walked towards the dressing room trying to keep her balance intact.

It was 2.30 am now and she had passed the state of being tipsy, she was drunk, giggling and laughing at everyone and everything in the dressing room.

"Are you all right Jordan?" The house mom asked.

"Oh yeah, don't worry about me mommy. I am great!"

"Can't believe you're still here" Gaby had walked in. "Where are you going from here?"

"I don't know, home I guess."

Suddenly, there was a phone ringing. It was Gaby's. She answered it and started smooth talking the guy on the line.

"Yeah, I will see you outside…I am talking to her right now. We're getting changed. Stay by the phone and I will call you right back." She turned around and smiled at Jordan. "A friend of mine is throwing a party at his house, do you want to come?" "Do I know him?" Jordan asked.

"Kind of!" was the answer. "It will be fun for sure, and on the good side is still early."

2.30 am! Time was different in gentlemen's clubs. Even after a week, Jordan had already understood that. The girls never went to sleep before 5 am and never woke up before noon.

"I don't know," she whispered, "where does he live?"

"Close to here," Gaby said, "a couple blocks down the road, come on, it will be fun, I promise."

"I'm not sure, I promised to meet Justin outside, but we'll see. Are you leaving now too?"

Gaby just laughed. Of course, she was leaving. She had put her jeans on already and her little sexy dress was stashed away in her locker. She could see Jordan was a little drunk, but she didn't say anything, as that made her even more fun. She had to convince her to come to the party, because she'd promised her friend to bring Jordan at any price.

"What did he see in Jordan that was so special?" she wondered. Ok she was blonde and pretty, but so was she, 'Ms. Jessica Rabbit'. Her phone rang again.

"Hello… yes, we are coming, see you in a second."

She put the phone down and turned to Jordan again, blocking her way between the lockers.

"So, are you coming?"

"Let's get out of here and I'll let you know outside. I need to check in with Justin first." Jordan replied.

They were both dressed now. Gaby, wearing jeans and a t-shirt, looking like any other 22 year old girl. The only sign of her job were her fake eyelashes and her big boobs.

"Are you not taking those off?" Jordan asked, pointing to her lashes. She pulled them off with her fingers.

"Doesn't it hurt? I can't imagine wearing those on every night. But it must be a matter of time till you get used to it, I guess."

"Lucky you, you don't need them. It's weird looking at you now Jordan, you don't look like you belong here."

Jordan turned around and checked her reflection in the mirror. She looked at the young girl staring at her. It was hard to believe sometimes that it was her! She was dressed in a baby pink track suit that she'd bought in 'Express' a week ago. Her hair was in a tight ponytail on the back of her head. She had no makeup on, besides her shiny lip gloss.

"I look like I'm 16 years old." She had turned 26 in February, "Not that I am moaning about it." She laughed.

"Come on sexy, let's get out of here and get rocking!"

Chapter 2

It was a chilly early September night. There was no wind, but it had definitely rained earlier, because you could feel the moisture in the air. Jordan closed up the zipper of her jacket and put on a pink baseball cap.

"Pretty in pink" said the bodyguard at the front door, who was checking her out.

"Have a good night, ladies." She smiled at him and he smiled back.

"So, what now?" Jordan said and then just at that moment her phone buzzed. It was Justin.

"Hi sweetie," his voice came through. "Listen, we're all going to my place. Why don't you jump in a cab and tell him to take you to 43rd and 2nd."

"I'll see you there... Hey, I have my girlfriend with me, is that all right?"

"Sure." he said.

She smiled and put the phone down. Justin was a real sweetheart. They had met the first night she'd started at the club.

He was very close to the boss, so it was handy having him as friend, just in case she ended up in any trouble.

"So, Gaby, you want to come with me? After hours at Justin's!" Gaby was on the phone as well, talking to her mystery friend.

"If you don't show up right now, we are gone" she said dryly and hung up, then looked at Jordan and answered her question "I do!... Let's get a cab. You got the address?"

They walked down the street and stopped at the corner of 60th for a taxi.

"Maybe I should better go home," Jordan said, looking at the building on the other side of the street, 'One Sutton place' her new home. The traffic light was on red, so she stared at it for a few seconds, seriously considering the choice of blowing the whole party idea and going home instead. A yellow taxi stopped right next to her at the very moment she was about to open her mouth and say to her friend "I changed my mind, I'm going home." She looked at the driver and said instead "What's meant to be, should be!!!..."

She gave the address to the driver and sat in the back of the car, still waiting for Gaby to get in, who was turning around, as if she was expecting someone.

"Get in the car, love!" she yelled at her, just as she heard tires screeching.

"Finally," Gaby whispered under her breath.

The creator of the chaos was a brand new shiny Mercedes convertible that had come from behind them on 1st Avenue and blocked the taxi in the middle of the road.

"What do you think, you are doing? I'm calling the police!" the driver yelled.

"What the hell is happening?" Jordan thought and looked out of the window.

"I can't believe that!" she said aloud. She couldn't believe her eyes. It was the drunk idiot from the champagne lounge from earlier that night. Gaby's friend. Oh, dear Lord, and he was also driving. She only hoped he'd sobered up a bit, since he couldn't even talk earlier.

"That's my friend," Gaby replied "the one I told you about. The one having an afterhours party at his place."

The man was out of his car already, leaning on the open door of the taxi. He looked at the girl inside and put on his most charismatic smile.

"Come on, you've got to come!"

"I am sorry, but I have my own arrangements going on, maybe another time." Jordan replied, still trying to figure out what this was all about.

"No, no please, you need to come. It'll be fun, I got wine, vodka, anything and everything you want," he said in a panic.

"Sorry, my friends are waiting for me," she insisted, trying to push him away from the car.

"I must do something! I must stop her!" his mind was racing. What could he do to make her come?! And then it hit him, she was a stripper, right? Strippers are all about cash! So hopefully that'll work, but how should he tell her that in front of the cabby. He looked at her, then looked back at Gaby… "I have to do it" he thought.

"Hey listen, I am packing white and green," he said.

Jordan, didn't get it at first. She looked at him, puzzled.

"I'm packing white and green" he repeated and fixed his eyes on hers.

Suddenly she realized what he meant. He was offering her money to go to party with him and drugs were on the table. He had got her attention now.

"That's something new!" she burst into a laugh. She only hesitated for a second, then pulled a 10 dollar bill from her bag and handed it to the driver.

"Sorry for wasting your time. I changed my plan and my destination."

If she only knew how she'd changed her life, she would've never have gotten out of that taxi.

Chapter 3

The car was going down 3rd avenue towards 45th street. Jordan was sitting in the back, while Gaby was sitting in the front next to Nicholas. They were busy, opening a pack of cocaine already...

"What the fuck am I doing here?" she asked herself. "I am drunk, high, going to somebody's house, without even knowing the guy..."

"Be careful please," she cried out from the back, as she could swear he was the worst driver she'd ever met... Gaby, reached over and gave her some of the white stuff...

"Well, let the party begin!" they both laughed.

Nick wasn't talking at all. He was focused on the road in front and the only thing that was distracting him was the image in the mirror, of the girl sitting in the back of his car. He smiled to himself. Sometimes things just happened when you were least expecting them.

Jordan was loosening up a bit. She was laughing over something with Gabriela and Nick couldn't take his eyes of her.

The way her lips were moving, the sound of her voice, the way her eyes were shining. That girl was amazing.

The Torch Building was situated on the corner of 3rd avenue and 45th street. The door attendant smiled when he saw the party of three coming in.

"How are you man?" Nick asked "I am not here for anyone, if anyone asks, is that clear, my friend? Come up in 15 minutes and I'll make you a drink."

The elevator closed and they disappeared. Nick's apartment was on the 36th floor, a beautiful one bedroom bachelor pad, with a big terrace and a breathtaking view. There were scented candles everywhere. A light brown leather sofa was in the middle of the living room, a glass coffee table in front of it. The big flat screen TV was on the wall. Jordan looked around curiously. She really liked the place. There were paintings everywhere on the walls, all in a unique style. Nicky boy was an art lover, or they could have belonged to an exgirlfriend.

Exgirlfriend, of course…it was easy to guess that if he was married, or had a girlfriend, they would not still be here. She looked at the flowers with surprise and then decided to touch them first before saying anything.

Fake! How pathetic! Jordan hated plastic flowers.

The host disappeared behind the bar in the open kitchen and showed up with three glasses and a shaker.

"I used to bartend," he said, "so what can I mix for you ladies?" "I'll take a Cosmo," Jordan said.

"For me, the same, and a tequila shot!" Gaby added.

"So, what's your name again?" Jo asked, "We were never properly introduced actually."

"Nicholas Walters, and you?"

"Isabelle Lucardi" Jordan said.

"I thought you were Jordan." he replied.

"That too, but only in Scores. I use Jordan as a stage name."

"Nice to meet you Isabelle."

"Same here, Nick"

"Where are the drinks? I'm so thirsty, need some water as well," Gaby said.

They all sat around the table, sipping the cocktails. There was an awkward silence in the room, then Nick threw down another pack of coke on the table. The candles were burning, George Michael was playing in the background and all three were deeply engaged in a conversation. Nick was trying to keep up an equal chat with both girl but, it was obvious his attention was mostly focused on Isabelle.

It had to be 4 o'clock in the morning and she was getting really tired, but thanks to the drugs and the alcohol, her mind was still racing, and her brain would not shut down. She was feeling exhausted…like an over loaded computer.

Nick was mixing the next drink when she suddenly glanced at him and after a second, she had to look at him again with her eyes wide open. It seemed to her as if she had just noticed him for the first time. She knew he was there, she had been talking to him, was in his house, been in his car but she'd never really noticed him. And now suddenly here he was. She looked at him again and their eyes locked.

"You're fucking handsome," she managed to say.

"And you're beautiful," he answered.

She felt embarrassed. It was as if she had just woken up from a deep sleep and only now started to register what was really happening around her… and there he was… six foot tall with a well-trained body, broad shoulders, chestnut brown hair, and these amazing, huge green eyes that were staring at her. She started to feel uncomfortable. She should go. Go, run away as far as she could and as quickly as she could. She could feel it in her heart, this man could be dangerous for her. This man could break the protective shield she had built around herself these last two years, and destroy her inner peace. He could control her feelings and emotions and either make her the happiest woman in the world or break her heart for always.

Nick sensed something was going on in her head and sat next to her.

"Are you alright?" he asked with a smooth voice, touching her hand.

Oh, God, he has been waiting for that, since the first moment he saw her. There was a chill going through his body. He could feel her emotions. She was so perfect.

"I am tired. I think I should go home. It's late already anyway" she said.

"You're scared of me, aren't you? I can feel it… but why? You know, I've got the strange feeling, that we are so much alike! It's in the air. I can read your thoughts, feel your emotions. I have never felt something like that."

She froze on the spot. She knew it, she knew it! He was dangerous and if that wasn't enough, he even knew he was dangerous. What has she done? Why did she come here? She should really leave as soon as she can. Her hands were shaking, she looked at him, her eyes filled with fear.

"I really need to go."

"Don't run away please," he said.

"I am not running away," she couldn't even look at him.

Oh yes, she was scared to face this gorgeous man and look again into his amazing eyes. He was so self confident, so sure about everything he did and said. His voice was smooth and strong at the same time. She wondered what it would be like if he kissed her. She was burning from the desire to touch his face.

"Then let us have another drink" he said, "would you like another Cosmo?"

"Hey, Nick, you fancy a shot" Gaby felt left out.

So Nick disappeared again and came back with three shot glasses and a tequila bottle.

"Chilled?" he asked.

"Yeah baby!"

He poured the liquor, and they all made a toast. "For us and for the great night we are having!" Nick looked at Isabelle.

"To us!" he added without the other girl hearing him.

Isabelle looked back at him without saying a word. What was she going to do with him? Her heart was beating double time. He leaned towards her and whispered in her ear, "You know, you can run and hide, but you can't escape your destiny! And stop asking yourself, why you are here, honey! Things happen for a reason!"

His words echoed in her ears long after he had stopped talking.

"I like you too" she said as she faced him, "…and I've got a strange feeling we could be more than just two strangers who've met under these circumstances. We could become more to each other than just a one night stand. So here's the deal. Call me a taxi. I will go home but I would really love to see you again."

Before he even could say anything, she reached for her bag, got out a piece of paper and wrote her phone number on it.

"Call me when you wake up tomorrow."

He looked at her, hesitating for a minute, wondering what the best way would be to stop her, to make her stay a little longer and then he came up with the decision. She was right. She was right. He had to be patient because he didn't want her just for now, he wanted her forever. So he could have all of time to spend with her. Why would he rush things now? No, she was right, and he would let her go. For now!

He looked at the piece of paper with her number. He better never lose this. He knew exactly what to do. He would write it on ten different notes and put them all around the house. Like that it could never been lost. But first things first. He saved the number in his phone.

"All right, I will call you a cab. Where are you going to?"

"61st street and 1st Avenue."

"You don't live far. We are almost neighbors," he smiled.

She really liked him. He was handsome, charming, successful… judging by his car and apartment. Oops, she didn't even know what he did for a living, the thought crossed her mind.

"I am a broker," he said.

"Can you really read my mind?"

"Not really, but I just saw you taking in the surroundings and read the expression on your face."

"Well, you are right. That was exactly what I was thinking. So, you're a broker, that's great. Not that I'm that familiar with that, but I know one thing for sure… the stock market is not boring!"

"No, it's not."

"OK, my taxi should be here by now. You all have a great night!" She turned towards Gaby. "I'll talk to you soon," she said with a wink.

She opened the door and headed towards the elevator.

He was looking at her with a big smile on his face. She smiled too. He came after her. The elevator was there now, and she had to go, but he couldn't resist the temptation and gave her a little kiss on her lips before the elevator door closed and left him alone in the hallway.

"Things happen for a reason" he thought with a smile and walked back into his apartment.

Chapter 4

It was two in the afternoon, when Isabelle woke up the next day. The afternoon sun was shining right into her eyes. It was a bright September day. She should have been out, doing things, enjoying the weather. She sat up in her bed and all the memories of the night before came back.

She smiled, neither angry nor upset with herself. Her head was hurting, but besides that, she was a happy girl. She looked out of the window over the Queensboro Bridge and started singing "it's a wonderful, wonderful life". From her bedroom window, she could see all the way down to Queens. All the rooms in the flat had floor to ceiling windows. That was important to her, not only for the view, but for the light as well. Isabelle had grown up in Spain and was used to the outdoor life. She loved the sun and not having enough light in the house made her very sad.

It was so nice of Frank to let her to move in with him. She'd met Frank years ago in London and it was by complete accident that she'd seen him in the club last Friday. She was embarrassed at first, him seeing her dancing in a strip club, but she quickly brushed it off. They'd talked. He'd been surprised to see her in New York. She'd told him she had no definitive plans for how long she was going to stay in the city or what she was going to do. When she mentioned she was going to have a look at a couple of studio apartments the day after, he smiled and said "Why don't you come and have a look at my place. It's a big two bedroom. You can have your own room, with your own bathroom. I just furnished it last month."

She looked at him and her mouth dropped open.

"Really? What about your family?" from what she knew, Frank was happily married with two kids.

"They're all in Florida. I moved my family there last summer. My head office is still in LA, that's where I spend most of my time. I got this apartment here, because for the last eight months, we were getting lots of new clients from New York and I was coming to the city almost every week, for a day or two. You know, I hate hotels, and I got tired of living out of a suitcase, so I rented the apartment six months ago. When I'm not here, it stays empty, so you're more than welcome to use it. And the best thing for you is that the building is just across the street. One block from here."

"I can't believe that, are you serious?" she asked, holding her breath.

"Hundred percent. Listen, why don't you come tomorrow and have a look. What time do you have to be here, in the club?"

"7:30 in the evening."

"I'll meet you at 6:30 pm, in my place. You can have a look and after that, we can go and have a quick drink somewhere around here."

"Sounds perfect to me." she answered in disbelief.

The first real shock was after the taxi had dropped her in front of the building. She'd stepped a few steps back to have a proper look at it.

"64 east 61st street" the address was right. She wanted to jump and scream with excitement. It was a brand new, black glass building. It had a doorman, a concierge, and a security guy. All three of them, were staring at her now.

"I'm going to see Mr. Green, he's expecting me." "Yes Ma'am." the concierge said.

The doorman walked her to the elevator.

Frank was waiting for her upstairs. The door was open. She entered and froze.

The place was unbelievable. This was for sure, the best apartment she'd seen lately. There was so much light coming in from all around. The place looked like a glass palace. The flooring was a warm colored wood. There was a cognac colored three seater leather couch in the living room, a large antique table in front of it and a big comfortable armchair on the other side of the table, right next to the windows. There was a small coffee table next to the chair with an antique lamp on that. On the other side of the bright room there was an enormous leather desk with a computer and some papers spread around.

"Do you want to see the rest of it?" Frank asked, amused by the expression on her face.

Everything was so exclusive in this place, even to the smallest details.

"Would you like a glass of wine?" he offered.

"Yes please," she said and followed him into the kitchen. Everything was perfect and shiny there too. Frank got a bottle of Chardonnay out of the fridge and poured them each a glass.

"To a happy living together," he smiled.

Frank was about forty years old. A big, tall man, over 6 ft and around 200 pounds. He had a very pleasant face and a warm smile.

"So this is the master bedroom" he said, entering a room, to the left of the living room. There was a huge king size bed, with a chest at the end of it, on top of which was a slick 60 inch Samsung HD TV. There was a walking closet, but the door was closed, so she couldn't check that one out. Floor to ceiling windows again and right in front of the window there was another desk, like the one in the living room only smaller. There was a big computer screen on it and a small Dell laptop to the side.

"How many computers do you need?" the question shot out of her mouth before she could stop it. "I am in the internet business, remember?" "Right," she smiled.

Frank was in the 'emails business'. Most of the biggest illustrated magazines were his costumers. He sorted and organized their email correspondence with their customers. It worked more or less like this, if you sent an email to Vogue magazine, it would actually go to Frank's Company, who would forward it to Vogue magazine. She wasn't good with computers, so she wasn't sure if she really understood what Frank's Company really did. Not that it actually mattered to her, so she continued to explore the room. She saw there was a printer combined with a scanner on the side of the desk too, and said, "Wow, you're pretty well connected, aren't you?"

"That's my job! C'mon let me show you your room."

They went back to the living room, through the kitchen and he opened the door right across from the main entrance.

It was a nice bright room, relatively smaller than the one she just saw but perfect for her. There was a comfy looking queen size bed in the middle, with two night tables on either side of it. There was a big lamp on the one on the right, a mirror on the wall to the right of the bed and two paintings of half naked bodies hanging on the wall behind the bed. The left side was all glass, like all the rest of the apartment. There was an open closet, not half as big as the one in Frank's room, but then again, more than enough for her. The bathroom was next door. Black marble on the floor and white on the walls. A bathtub and a shower. She took a deep breath, turned around to Frank and looked straight into his eyes.

"Frank you're in trouble!" she said.

"Why? What's wrong?"

"You're never going to get me out of this apartment. You'll have to call the police to drag me out!"

He laughed, delighted, and raised his glass of wine.

"Here's to a happy together living and a long-term friendship," he said.

The next day she moved in.

Chapter 5

The phone rang, it was almost 5 o'clock in the afternoon. It was Paris, her girlfriend from Scotland.

"Where were you last night? I was looking for you and I have a steamy story to tell you" Isabelle said.

"Oh babe, I was so tired yesterday. You know I've been working every night since I got here. I needed to catch up on some sleep, but tell me, how was it last night? Did you make any money?"

"I did all right. One thousand five hundred bucks, but after I paid the house and all the rest, I ended with one thousand, two. That's good huh!"

"What are you doing now? You want to go for a drink before work?"

"I rather stay in. Why don't you come here? I have a bottle of wine."

"I'll be on my way in about half an hour. I'll give you a call when I'm in the lobby. Okay? Love you babe. Go get yourself ready."

"Love you too," she put the phone down and looked dreamily out of the window.

She'd been thinking about last night and couldn't wait till April, Paris' real name, was there, so she could share the whole story with her and hear somebody else's opinion about Nick…who still hadn't called her! Has he's forgotten all about her, she thought. They were both very drunk last night and on top of it all they were doing drugs, so normally these two trick your mind and change the reality of the moment. But if that was so, why couldn't she stop thinking about him?

"Thank God I didn't get his cell number, because with my temper and lack of patience, I would have called him 25 times already. This way I can play it cool, like I don't care" she thought "…or like I don't have any other possibility…can't call someone without a number, can I?!" She took another sip of her coffee and looked out of the window again.

"Better get myself ready for work before April shows up" she thought and went to take a shower.

"I'm here!" April sang down the phone "please, tell your sexy doorman to let me in."

Isabelle took the phone receiver that was connected directly to the front desk.

"Let her in" she said briefly.

She hated the door attendant from the front desk. First of all, it was a woman. And secondly, she had never seen her smile. Always angry at the world, she looked like she hadn't had sex for at least six years and had never received flowers in her entire life.

The doorbell rang.

"Hi honey, I've missed you" April cried out.

Isabelle had only met her a week ago, but they had been inseparable since. They helped each other at work and went for lunches together during the day. April was Scottish but was living in London. She was 5ft 4"tall and about 110lbs. Her amber skin was a very exotic match with her Scottish accent. She had long black hair and the color of her eyes changed everyday depending on her mood. She used colored contact lenses. Today she had blue eyes. If she didn't talk too much, as most of it was of no interest to anyone, she could be really a great girl. But nobody was perfect, and neither was April. She always had to be right about everything, about everybody, never made a mistake and she could not sit still longer than two minutes. She was the most hyper person Isabelle had ever met. Being around her was lots of fun but could also be demanding work, putting up with her constantly changing moods. Anyway, that was the best friend Isabelle could have at the moment and she was starting to really like that crazy Scottish girl.

"So where's my drink?" April said, throwing her bag on the couch and lighting up a cigarette straight away.

"You know Frank doesn't like smoking and he has asthma."

"Open a window! You got enough of them, don't you?"

Isabelle smiled and gave her a glass of wine. There was no point in arguing with her. That's the way April was, and no one would ever change her.

She sat on the couch next to her and lit herself a cigarette too. At least when she opens a window, it won't be for just one cigarette. On the other hand, she knew already that if they spent an hour here it would be more than two cigarettes anyway.

"So, what's the steamy story you wanted to tell me on the phone?" April asked.

"Don't tell me you're all loved up with one of your clients please. You got to stop thinking with your heart and start using your brain. Think money, money, money!"

"Do you want to hear the story, or do you want to keep on guessing it?"

"Go on, I'm listening!"

Isabelle told her everything that had happened the night before. All the details and all the thoughts that had been going through her head. She was almost coming to the end when her friend yelled out…

"Oh my god I know who he is. He's a young guy, isn't he? I'd say something around 30?"

"29!"

"Same thing. I was right. I know who he is. He was with Gaby a couple of weeks ago…right? And he spent about three thousand dollars! And they were sniffing cocaine in the private room" she lit another cigarette. "…and you like that guy…?"

She made a strange face as if she was about to ask "are you alright in the head?" Or "did you get hit by a truck yesterday?" Or "did someone brainwash you?"

"I think I do" Isabelle said, at that very moment her cell rang. There was no number on the display. "Strange" she thought.

"Hello, hi, it's Nicholas Walters from last night. How are you today?"

"Oh my God, it's him" she said putting her hand over the phone so he couldn't hear her.

She jumped up off the couch and started walking in circles around the table.

"What do I do? What do I do?" she looked at April hoping to get an advice.

"Talk to him." April answered.

"Ah hi, I'm fine. Have a little headache but everything else is all right. Did you make it to work today?"

"Ah don't even ask. I just left the office," he said.

She glanced at her watch it was almost 6:30pm.

"I can't count how many cups of coffee I drank today, and I still feel dead. Can't wait to get home, have a shower and lay in front of the TV. An early night for me tonight. What about you, gorgeous?"

"I am at home with a girlfriend of mine having a glass of wine and after that we are going to work. That's alright with me though, because I slept till 2 pm… Poor you, you must have gone straight to work?"

"You said it, but listen, I'll give you a call later this week and if you want, we can meet for a drink if that's fine with you!" "Let's do that," she said shortly.

Somehow, she was expecting him to ask if he could see her tonight or now, even. She'd been thinking about him since she woke up and he's talking about later this week…

"Ok babe, I'll talk to you soon. Give me a call when you want to meet for a drink. I gotta go now."

She put the phone down. Her smile had faded from her face, and she looked like she was about to cry.

"Aha!" April jumped in.

"I knew it! I knew it! You're loved up with that Nicki boy! But don't worry, it'll pass."

"I'm not in love with him. I don't even know him. I like him, but that's all."

"Honey, what do you want from that guy? Yes, he's young and pretty, but would he pay your mortgage? Would he support you or pay the money you owe? No, all he wants is to get you in bed and have some fun and I know you will let that happen, but don't let him upset you. Pull yourself together and start smiling again. We need to be at work in half an hour and I can guarantee you no one will be willing to sit with you if you show up there with that sad face. C'mon smile... smile for me please. Have a drink, have a cigarette and smile.

Chapter 6

It was early the next afternoon when Frank rang.

"Hello there, how are you? I'm flying into New York today and wondered if you have any plans for the evening?"

"I'm going to work later on, but besides that, no, I have no plans"

"If it's okay with you, I'll be home at 5 o'clock and we can go grab something to eat. We can go to D'Agostino round the corner, or you prefer to go to La Scalinatella on 62th and 3rd Avenue? I know it's your favorite restaurant in the area."

"Let's just meet at 5 pm in the apartment and take it from there."

"Perfect, my driver is picking me up at 4:15 from La Guardia, so I won't be later than 5pm. See you then."

She'd been really lazy today, watched all the soap operas, went to the bank to deposit her money and laid around the rest of the day. Didn't even check her emails. She wasn't in a good mood, but she didn't really know why. It would definitely be a good idea to get out of the house.

Frank was lots of fun and always motivated her somehow. Ah, and Frank was a lover of fine and expensive wines, as was she. Tonight, she would order a bottle of Tignanello and forget about all the insignificant things that had driven her crazy lately. It couldn't be that her mood has been so affected by that guy Nick, could it?!

She had already forgotten about him, Nicholas who…

The phone rang again. It was April. She only looked at it and went to take a shower. Really not ready for the "yes I knew it and I told you so…" conversation right now. Besides she'd see her later at work anyway.

"What's wrong with me?" she thought "why do I feel so lonely and unhappy? Need to do something about it. I hate being miserable. And I hate it even more when there is no actual reason for feeling this way."

Frank arrived exactly at 5pm, always on time, never late. Isabelle always enjoyed the times when he was in New York. They decided to have a bite to eat in La Scalinatela and after that stop for a drink at Merchants. It was all in the area. That was another great thing about the apartment. Right next to the club and surrounded by the best restaurants from the upper east side of Manhattan.

La Scalinatella was a small Italian place with an amazing kitchen and exclusive wine list. They walked down the 61st street to the 3rd avenue. She was still feeling miserable.

"So how is work going?" Frank asked. "Do you know what your plans will be, or you are still just going with the flow?"

"I don't know Frank. I miss Europe, especially Spain, but it's going to be winter there soon, and Mallorca is not exactly the most exciting place to be for the winter. On the other hand, I heard it's lots of fun in New York and the girls in the club say it's the best time to make money…all the way from now till past Christmas."

"That's fine with me. You can stay in the apartment, as long as you want."

They sat at the corner table in the restaurant. It was early, so they didn't need a reservation. First things first, Isabelle thought…

"Shall we get a bottle of Tignanello?"

"Of course! Go on."

Frank really liked this girl. They always had a fun time together. He was shocked at first, when he saw her in the club, but what was bad about it. She was doing her best and he knew the girls in Scores were making crazy money. He knew her dad and that fact was a little embarrassing, but she'd made him promise he would never say a word to him. He liked having her living in the apartment. She was full of life, always excited about something and never giving up. Full of dreams and new ideas. She lit up the whole place with her presence. The other thing he really liked about her, was how neat and tidy she was.

"So, what else is new? You look a little bit down today. Sure you don't want to stay home tonight and take the night off from work?"

"I wish but I can't… You know I have all this money to pay back and I'm already late with the payment. I must work every night if I want to make it and I will. But don't worry, I'll be alright and if I start feeling really bad, I promise, I'll come home! Are you going to be in town tomorrow, or are you flying to Florida?"

"I have a few meetings in the morning and it depends, if I get everything done in the afternoon, I might get an evening flight and if not, I'll fly out the day after."

"That's cool! So, if you stay, we could make lunch again. I would like to go back to The Central Station, to that place where you took me last week."

"You mean Cipriani?"

"That's the one! I really like it there."

"Ok, if I stay, we go."

The waiter topped up her wine glass. She could feel the wine heating her blood. Oooh, she loved the taste of it! She finished her salad, sat back in her chair, looked back at Frank and smiled.

"I'm happy you're here, really!"

He looked in her eyes and knew she meant it. But what was wrong with her? She was looking sad. Maybe she was tired? That job she was doing wasn't easy. It could get you down.

"You know what, I have an idea. I'll be going to London on a business trip next month for a week and I'll be needing someone to come with me… Don't worry it's not what, you are thinking. I am going to meet clients for dinner, and it would look better if I have company. If you want, you're more than welcome to come with me and before you say anything… I know you need to pay money back, so how about I give you a check for 5,000 dollars."

She looked at him in disbelief. He saw the confusion in her eyes.

"You will have your own hotel room. Nothing to worry about. You'll probably even learn something about my business, and if you like it, I'll send you on intensive training program and you could start working for me. It won't be the money you're making in Scores, but you can't dance all your life anyway. That's a temporary situation. You need to start thinking about your future…and believe me there is no future in a strip club."

She was still staring at him, her eyes wide open.

"Are you serious, about what you're saying?"

"Yes, I am. I am flying on October 5th for six days. It's not even a full week. So, you want to come?"

She raised her glass for a toast. He did the same.

"To London" they both said and laughed.

"I'm feeling so much better" she said. "It's got to be either the wine or you, or both."

They finished their dinner and Frank asked for the bill. He didn't want to put her under unnecessary stress, as he knew she had to go to work.

"Thanks Frank, you're always so nice to me." She really meant it.

It was almost 8:30pm, by the time she got to the club. She was so excited about going to London, flying first class, going to all the nice places, and getting paid five thousand dollars on the top of it.

Probably while they were in Europe, she could invite Frank to Mallorca. Her dad would be there and Frank had promised to keep her job secret. Sounded like a great idea. She would take him around the island, show him the port and take him for a walk down into Palma. She was always so proud of her island. Mallorca was indeed a beautiful place. Laying in the Mediterranean Sea, it was part of the Balearics: Mallorca, Menorca, Ibiza and Formentera. It was a twenty-minute flight from Barcelona and just over an hour from Madrid.

"Hey honey, you're late" April showed up at the dressing room door and dragged her out of her dreams. She had come earlier and was already dressed, with full make up on. April loved her make up. "Your face is your passport!" was her favorite phrase. "Where have you been?"

"Dinner with Frank. We had to go over a couple of things."

"When am I going to meet him? You said, he would be my type. You think he'd like me too?"

She laughed and came closer. The scent of April's perfume was so strong it was hard to breathe next to her.

"Don't you suffocate all these men with your perfume? Girl, one day you'll kill someone and you'll get charged with murder! It would be all over the news... "...man dies in a strip club suffocated by dancer's perfume. A sweet way to die..." All the dancers in the dressing room laughed.

Isabelle picked out a silver-gray velvet dress out of her locker. Put it in front of her and looked in the mirror. It looked very elegant. A deep cut decolletage at the front and a naked back. She put a pair of fake Tiffany earrings and a fake diamond bracelet on her wrist.

"You need to put more make up on. It's dark outside remember. You need more color" April said, as she pulled out a brush and dipped it in a dark gold, shiny powder.

"Stay away from me" Isabelle cried, " Really, take that stuff way. I don't want it."

"Yes, you do, it will make your skin look a little darker. Look at you, you look like Casper the ghost."

"Yeah, probably next to you, I do!"

They both laughed, maybe because April was black.

Isabelle went regularly to a tanning salon, so there was no way she was white… and certainly not like Casper the ghost!!! She had a nice golden tan, which went perfectly with her honey blond hair. She turned around again to look at herself in the mirror and smiled with satisfaction. She looked great, and she knew it. She liked getting compliments and she liked giving people compliments if they deserved them. Casper the Ghost, my ass!!!

Chapter 7

They walked out of the dressing room and walked into the Jungle. That's what she called the showroom of Scores. There were a few tables occupied, but it wasn't crowded. It was only 9pm.

Men didn't go to strip clubs before eleven. Dinner first and then pleasure. Most people who came to the club were business people, bringing their business associates on a night out. It seemed to be that a gentlemen's club was the best place to close a deal.

"We should be getting percentages of what they make from each deal" thought Isabelle.

Her mind ran away to London again and she looked at April. Should she tell her about Frank's offer, or should she keep it to herself.

They walked around the room, gave a couple of dances and went to the bar to get a drink. A normal Thursday night.

A couple of hours later, Isabelle moved to the other side of the club, to the restaurant area. She sat down and started talking to Willow, the girl behind the bar. It had to be around midnight when she felt somebody watching her. She checked around. Nothing. April was sitting next to her, moaning about not making enough money. Isabelle wasn't really listening to her. She was busy with her own thoughts, and she couldn't get rid of the feeling, that someone was watching her. She tried to focus and find where the mystery one was sitting. Turning slowly and following her instincts… next to the wall, on the opposite side of the room, two men were sitting in black suits and ties, no older than 30. The one facing her, was staring directly in her direction. She took her martini glass and raised it to him, smiling and at that same second she recognized him. She almost dropped her drink. "Oh my God it's him!"

"Who? Where?" April asked.

"He's over there, third table next to the wall, two men, the one facing me is Nicholas Walters. The one, I told you about, the other night." She didn't wait to hear the answer.

Excitement spread all over her body. She was blushing. That man was making her heart beat fast and confusing her mind, even from the other side of the room. What should she do? Stupid question! They were in a strip club!

She took her glass and made her way in his direction, leaving April alone at the bar.

"Nice to see you again. I thought, you wanted to call me later this week!"

"I do, and I tried to call you earlier, but your phone went straight to mailbox. You can check your messages later."

He stood up, took her hand and gave her a kiss, which sent a heatwave through her body.

"I sure will," she said and took a seat next to him.

She felt like a schoolgirl, kissed for the first time.

"My friend Bradley and I were out and about in the area, and I thought… I might see you here."

"So, you were looking for me, because you've been missing me" she giggled.

He smiled without saying anything. They had a bottle of red wine on their table, so Nick offered her a glass.

"No thanks, I don't want to end up like the last time I met you." and they both laughed.

Bradley was getting bored at the table. Nick hadn't even introduced him to the girl, or her to him and now these two only had eyes for each other.

"I'll go check the showroom." he said to Nick.

"Ok buddy, I'll be here." he answered, without even looking at him.

Nick was trying to absorb every little detail of Isabelle's face. He remembered she was pretty, but he had to admit she was a lot prettier than he remembered. Her skin was flawless and her eyes were glistening. Her smile could melt the iceberg that took down the Titanic. Her voice was like music in his ears.

The waiter passed by, and he ordered a shot of tequila for himself. He still could remember, she didn't like tequila.

"So where are you from?" he asked "You never told me anything about you. You're definitely not American, even though you speak perfect English. Your accent is hard to define, where you come from."

"Not from this world." she flattered her eyelashes "I'm from Venus."

He wanted to kiss her so badly.

"I'm a little cold," she whispered in his ear.

He took his jacket and put it around her shoulders, then pulled her to him and gave her a kiss on her cheek. She blushed again and wished the earth could've opened up and swallowed her. She didn't want him to see the effect he was having on her. Her heart was jumping in her chest. She finished her drink and asked for another one.

"It's over," she thought "I'm getting drunk again tonight!" She was feeling so nervous she needed the alcohol to calm her down.

They'd been sitting at that table probably for an hour and a half, when Isabelle suddenly remembered, she was here to make money and not fall in love. Isabelle could fall in love, Jordan not!

"Do you want to go for a dance?" she asked Nick.

"No, I'm fine here with you."

"Well, let's go to the private room then, I'm getting bored here." she lied.

She could never get bored next to him. He looked at her and his expression changed.

"Are you trying to take me for my money?" he asked.

"Not for all of it, but for some of it, yes" she answered promptly, looking straight into his eyes, trying to read his thoughts and figure out his reaction.

"Hey, listen, I know you're here for the money but…"

"I'm not here just for the money" she interrupted him "but I do work here. And I have bills to pay."

She'd got right to the point. He didn't know what to tell her. He liked her a lot but he didn't want to pay her for being there with him. On the other hand, that's how it worked in places like this. Oh, he was feeling uncomfortable and confused. There had to be a way out of this situation. He didn't want her to leave. He didn't want to pay her. He didn't want her to get upset or angry… so how could he deal with all that together under the same roof?

"Let me pay the bill here" he said, "and then we can go to the champagne VIP lounge." He pulled out his credit card and put it on the table.

"Don't worry, you'll get what you want, but you're not getting me in any of these backrooms. It's better I give this money to you, than make the owner of the club any richer." He had a point!

They got the bill and went to the VIP lounge. It was crowded there. They asked for a table but there was no chance. Nick saw his friend, Bradley, sitting with a couple of girls in the corner, he grabbed Isabelle's hand and they both went to say hello. The whole idea was to get a seat at the table, and it worked. They ordered shots for everyone.

"Am I getting a dance now or what?"

She laughed and got up. Isabelle was a good dancer. She loved music and she could move in a very sexy way. He didn't have to ask her twice.

"Don't take off your dress. I think you're sexy enough with your dress on."

"As you wish Mr. Walters."

She leaned closer to him, pulling her hair around her face, hiding his under it as well, and stopped like that for a long second. She could feel his breath, his mouth was a hair's width away from her lips. It was hot. He could feel her excitement. Her breath getting shorter. So was his. If he only moved an inch, their lips would touch and then she could not give any more guarantees.

He wasn't sure about her, but she didn't seem to be very in control either. She was looking at his lips scared even to breathe. What would happen if she kissed him? No one could see them. Both their faces were well hidden under her long hair.

"No." She pulled away.

She could control herself. She was strong. She'd spent years, many years, working on herself and teaching herself, how to control her feelings and not to be manipulated by her emotions.

She moved a step back and started moving to the rhythm of the music.

Nick was staring at her like he was hypnotized, his eyes weren't blinking anymore. He wasn't thinking straight anymore. This woman was killing him. He couldn't recall desiring another woman, the way he wanted Isabelle in that second. He wished that all the people in the club would disappear, and it was only him and her. The way she was moving her body was driving him crazy. She came close to him and touched his ear with her lips, whispering something into it. He couldn't hear her.

"What? I'm sorry"

"Do you like it?" she whispered, and her cheek rubbed softly against his.

It seemed like time had stopped, and the air was filled with pure naked sexual desire. Nick was overheated. He took off his jacket and untied his tie. The song ended.

"Thank God" he thought.

Isabelle sat down on his lap laughing and put her arms around his neck, positioning her breasts right in front of his eyes.

"Is she doing that on purpose?" he thought, the blood pulsing in his head.

"Jordan!" one of the bouncers yelled out "get up right away before the manager sees you."

Strange rules for a strip joint but the girls were not allowed to sit in the guy's lap. So, she moved and sat next to him.

"Do you want one more?" she asked.

"One more what?"

"Another dance, silly."

"Oh no, no! That was great" he said and took his wallet out. He counted five hundred dollars and put it in her hand.

"That's for you," he said. "And I guess we are even for tonight." The smile on her face was saying everything without her even speaking a word.

"Thank you, babe. You are not leaving, are you?" He glanced at his watch, a Pasha, Cartier.

"It's almost two. I have to work tomorrow. I got to be in the office at 7am."

He didn't want to leave without her.

"What time do you finish tonight?"

"I'll see what I can do."

They looked at each other in silent understanding.

He watched her go through the room, stop next to the dressing room and talk to a guy wearing a dark suit and a walkie-talkie in his right hand. That had to be the manager, he thought. He could see from her gestures and facial expression, that the conservation was not going in a good way for her. A minute later she was back at the table.

"I'm leaving in twenty minutes!"

"Are you coming to my place?" he asked holding his breath. She looked at him with smiling eyes.

"What was the address again?"

Then they both left the table. He to the exit, she to the dressing room to get changed.

Chapter 8

The taxi dropped her off in front of the Torch tower. She entered the building, and the doorman came towards her.

"I'm here to visit Mr. Walters." Isabelle said.

"Yes, I know he has already called ma'am. And your name?"

"Isabelle, Isabelle Lucardi."

"Would you like to wait for Mr. Walters here, or you prefer to go upstairs?"

"I will wait upstairs, thanks a lot." The door was locked.

"Damn it." She thought.

It was too late to go back down. She didn't want to make herself look stupid in front of the doorman plus she stank of cigarettes and alcohol. She sat down on the floor, resting her back against the wall. She was tired. She closed her eyes for a second and tried to remember the moment they'd shared in the club.

Chapter 9

"Are you ok, Isabelle, wake up?" She could hear Nick's voice coming from somewhere far, far away... He was calling her name. She tried to open her eyes. At first it all looked quite blurry...

He was on his knees, shaking her shoulders and his voice was filled with worry.

"Yeah, what's happening?" she rubbed her eyes.

"You scared me to death" he whispered and moved gently the hair from her eyes.

"I fell asleep. Sorry Nick. I was only waiting for you and didn't want to be a problem babe. Sorry. I probably should've have gone home... How long have I been there?"

"About 10 minutes, but you were sleeping so deep, you weren't moving. I thought something had happened to you."

She could see in his eyes he was telling the truth. It warmed her heart. She couldn't resist the temptation, so she touched his face gently and pulled slowly his head to hers until their lips met in a passionate kiss.

Right there, in front of his door, in the lobby of his building he got to kiss her properly for the first time.

They looked at each other and he kissed her again, slowly exploring her mouth and kissing the corners of her lips. "Let's go" he said and opened the door.

She felt dizzy after the kiss and needed to sit down.

"Do you want a drink?"

"Just water please…No ice."

That was a European habit no one could break in her. She hated ice in the water. Liked it just the way it was. Clean and pure.

"What's that?" she pointed to a glass object she'd spotted that looked somewhat like a pipe.

"You've never seen a water pipe? It's for smoking pot" he explained to her.

"Smoking pot?"

"Grass! Marijuana!"

"Ah, ok."

"You don't smoke" he asked.

"Only cigarettes, never tried that stuff"

"So tonight will be your first time" he took the lighter from the table, put some grass in the little hole in the pipe and lit it up.

"You have to inhale it and hold your breath for a few seconds, then let it out. Do what I do."

He showed her how to do it and passed her the pipe. She took one puff of it and handed it back to him

"Do you feel something?"

"Not yet."

She was sitting on his couch, smoking pot for the first time and looking totally disorientated.

He pulled her gently to him, brushed her hair from her face and kissed her nose. She was silent, but he could see the fire starting to light up in her eyes. He kissed her slowly and smoothly, until he heard the little roar of pleasure she gave. She didn't know, if it was pleasure or pain, she knew only one thing for sure, his kiss gave her the biggest thrill her body had ever known. Too stunned to protest, she felt the strong sensation of him, the sound of his heartbeat against her breast and the hardness of his body enveloping her with his heat. His lips were firm now upon hers with hungry demand. He kissed her deeper and deeper until he took her breath away and everything started to spin around her. It was only a kiss, she thought. It was just a kiss that send a fire to her blood…What would happen after? The thought alone made her blood start to cook and made her shiver at the same time.

His hands moved up on her shoulders, and he tried to take off her t-shirt. She pushed him away, managed somehow to stand up from the couch and took his hand in hers. Her eyes were on fire her breath was short and her lips were swollen from his kisses.

"This way" he said and led her to the bedroom.

She started undressing herself while he was laying on the bed, his eyes locked on her. She was standing there completely naked, looking so perfect. He reached for her. His fingers went through her hair, and she saw the intense desire burning in his eyes. They were not green anymore but dark, really dark. He kissed her again and she got lost, somewhere between this world and heaven. It wasn't him and her anymore, it seemed like they become one. His hands were playing with her, running up and down her body. His touch was so gentle. She wanted him so much. He felt her desire and moved on top of her finding his way into her...

She closed her eyes and let herself enjoy every second of that journey to heaven.

They made love a couple of times that night, until they fell asleep in each other's arms. She could feel his arms around her the whole night and the warmth of his body behind her back. She had never felt that complete. It was a brand new experience for her.

Chapter 10

She woke up with a smile and looked around her. Still in his house but where was he. Probably in the office, she thought and looked at her watch 11:30am.

"Oh my God, I forgot about Frank."

She ran to the living room searching for her cell phone. It was laying on the couch. Four missed calls, two from Frank. She dialed the number and let the phone ring.

"Hello there, you are still alive? I didn't see your bag and your shoes this morning and I checked your room, but you weren't here. I got worried. Is everything all right?"

"Don't worry. I'm sorry I didn't let you know I wasn't coming home last night. I got wasted and ended up sleeping at April's. I just woke up and saw you'd called. Are we still up for lunch today?"

"Yes, my flight is leaving for Florida at 4pm, so I got enough time. I've scheduled one of my meetings at the Central Station for 1 o'clock. It will take only a few minutes then we can eat and I will go from there straight to the airport. Are you coming to the apartment first, or shall we meet at Cipriani?" Frank asked.

Isabelle looked at herself and sighed.

"I'm coming home. I need a shower and a change of clothes. Be there in twenty minutes."

She put the phone down and looked for her cigarettes. "What a night!" she thought.

She wished Nick was there. That man was amazing. She really liked him…but there was no time for daydreaming right now. She stank, she couldn't go out on the street like that.

She decided to take a quick shower there and do all the beauty stuff in her own bathroom. She fixed the bed and smiled at the thought of what they'd done in it last night.

Isabelle was just about to leave and was writing Nick a note when the door opened, and he entered the room.

"I thought you'd still be here," he said, smiling and gave her a kiss "did you sleep alright?"

"Like an angel" she kissed him back "I got to go back to my apartment, and I've got some things to do this afternoon." "When will I see you again?" he asked.

"Soon, very soon. By the way, you know I don't even have your cell phone number."

"You can have it" and he gave her his card.

"I'll give you a call. I'm doing a medical show in Waldorf Astoria this weekend, so I will be busy, but I'll find a way to catch up. I'll not be working in the club 'til Monday."

"What kind of a show is that?"

"It is a trade show for plastic surgeons, and I'll be working for one of the companies producing scalpels, scissors and all the stuff that plastic surgeons need. I'll be on their booth, trying to attract customers. They are paying me two and a half thousand dollars for the three days, plus I will have a room at the Waldorf Astoria during that time."

He looked at her, like he didn't believe her.

"I gotta go. I'll give you a call" she gave him a long, wet kiss and ran out of the door leaving him speechless and lonely in his apartment.

Lunch in Cipriani was great. She and Frank were laughing all the time.

"You are glowing today. What happened last night? Did you make a million dollars" Frank joked.

"No, I had the greatest sex in my life." she thought, but kept her thoughts to herself.

"I just feel good today… must be the weather."

After Frank left for the airport, she went back to the apartment.

She needed to take a bath and probably a nap… She wasn't sure, if she was going to work tonight. The medical show would start the next morning at 8 am, so she had to be there at 7.30am, which meant waking up at 6:30am.

"No, that will not fit in with working tonight" she thought.

She was asleep, in front of the TV, when the sound of her cell phone woke her up. It was Charles Parrish, owner of Parrish Surgical, the company she was working for tomorrow. He was supposed to arrive from Boston that evening, but she wasn't expected to be in the hotel until first thing tomorrow.

"Hi Isabelle, how are you?" Charly asked.

"Welcome back" she said "how was your trip?"

"It was ok. I took a nap in the limousine on the way to New York, so I'm rested. I just checked into the hotel, and they told me you are still not here!" his voice was showing his worry "is something wrong or you going to turn up later?"

"I'm sorry Charly, I thought I was due first thing tomorrow, but if you need me, I can be there in an hour." She looked at her watch 6pm.

"Yes" he said on the other line. "It would be better if all of our crew is here, so there'll be no complications tomorrow morning."

"You're right. Give me an hour, I'll call you from my room, after I've checked in."

She was about to put the phone down, when she heard his voice, "By the way, me and the docs are going out to Town for dinner, would you like to join us?" "Sure" she said.

Charly was a very handsome man, around 36 years old, coming from a very wealthy and conservative family, born and raised in Boston. He had graduated in Harvard and achieved a business degree. Most of his friends were doctors and his best friend Dr. Jay Lucas was a plastic surgeon specializing in face lifting and nose surgery.

The birth of 'Parrish Surgical' had been two years ago, when Charly had come up with the idea to combine Jay Lucas's knowledge about surgery and his own family knowledge about metals and hard materials.

"Put both these together to create a product, better than anything that the market has to offer and produce it in the family factory! Keep it in the family!" That was Charly's motto.

The first time Isabelle met Charly, she was very attracted to him. They'd met on a rainy day, three weeks ago, at the traffic lights on 5th avenue and 56th street. Neither of them had an umbrella and were soaked to the skin. He'd looked at her and laughed while she gave him an angry look.

"It's not funny" she'd said.

After seeing him all wet as well, she had to laugh too. He'd invited her for a drink, and they'd ended up having lunch in 'Bice Cucina'.

He told her his story, while she listened not telling him anything about herself. She didn't have a story to tell. She was from Europe, was living in a three star hotel looking for a job, like any other of the 8 million people in that city… it was too nice of an afternoon to spoil it… So, she blew it out of her mind and listened to him.

He wasn't tall, but very sporty. Dark black hair, dark eyes and dark complexion. There was something exotic about him. It came up later in the conversation that his father's side of the family was Greek.

Charly was very well spoken and had fine manners. A real gentleman.

He'd come back into town a week later and they'd had lunch again. It was last week when he called her and offered her the job for the coming weekend. She knew he'd done that first of all, and if not only, because he liked her and not just as a friend, but she hadn't cared… not until now… Not until she'd met Mr. Walters.

"To hell with him" she thought and tried to push away the image of Nick from her head. She really didn't have the time and energy to think about him. And she would focus and ignore these stupid emotions, which were dancing in her heart. She had always done it and she'll do it again. He was just another man nothing more!

She got up from the couch and went to the bathroom to get ready for the Waldorf Astoria, and dinner that evening with Charles and his friends. She looked in the mirror and smiled. There was no man in this world that was going to make her lose focus. No one... not even Nicholas Walters. That was the way she liked herself. Strong, concentrated, self confident, always independent. She would never be like any of those crying women who were weeping their whole life away over a man.

Chapter 11

She was wearing a grey suit from Jill Sanders. Isabelle loved fashion and had a very exclusive taste in clothes. Her hair was blow-dried straight, and she was looking hundred percent like a business woman when she showed up at the reception desk of the Waldorf Astoria. The moment she walked into her room, she called Charles.

"The room is beautiful, thank you very much" she said.

"I'm glad you like it. We are meeting downstairs at the bar in half an hour."

"Perfect, I'll see you there" she turned on the TV and laid down on the sofa. She had half an hour to kill.

Her mind went back to the night before. She could still feel Nick's hands over her body and the burn of his kisses.

"I have to get him out of my thoughts" she thought... "Should I call him?"

It was a quick switch of mind. Her phone rang. It was April again. She hadn't really had time for her lately. They should catch up next week.

"I've been trying to call you all day. You vanished off the face of the earth. Last time I saw you, you were all loved up with that broker guy of yours, Nicholas Walters."

"I slept with him," it jumped out of her lips.

"What?" April screamed so loud, Isabelle had to pull away from the phone.

"You slept with him? Girl, are you crazy? What do you want from this guy? He can barely pay his own bills. I told you think money, money, money. I can't believe you've done that."

There was a long pause and then her voice came again. "How was he?"

"Amazing" Isabelle answered. "I want to see him again, but I'm stuck for the weekend. I told you about the med show, didn't I?"

"Yes, you did honey. Stop wasting your time and energy on that Nick. Concentrate. I'll come and see you tomorrow during the day. Then you can introduce me to all these beauty surgeons. I'll probably find someone to fix my boobs! I want them big. I got to go." And she was gone.

"Stop wasting your time" echoed back in Isabelle's ears. She only had sex with him for God's sake, she didn't say she wanted to marry him.

She looked at her phone, fighting the temptation to call him and decided to go downstairs to the bar instead.

The guys didn't show up until 8.15 pm. There were four of them. Charles Parrish, his friend and partner in Parrish Surgical, Jay Lucas, his best friend Grant Hamilton and another friend, a plastic surgeon, Frank Merit. Charles introduced Isabelle to everyone.

It was awkward being the only female in the group, but it had its pros as well. She was getting all the attention the whole evening.

They went to 'Town' on 56th street and 5th avenue for dinner and after, they walked all the way down to the Hyatt hotel. There was an open air bar and the weather was still good for sitting outside. At least she could smoke there, she was happy about their choice.

Charles had been very nice to her, giving her tons of compliments. Now she knew for sure he did like her. It wasn't hard to miss it. It was clear to everyone at the table.

They were all having a great time. Everybody was laughing and making jokes. She was happy she'd accepted the invitation.

They didn't come back to the hotel until after midnight. Charles walked her down to her room and gave her a goodnight kiss on the cheek.

"I'll see you tomorrow at breakfast" he said, "I'll call to wake you up."

She hesitated for a moment… should she invite him in…? He was too much of a gentleman to ask for it or push his way in.

"Don't waste your time" echoed in her ears again. "Well, he's married, so if I invite him in, that would for sure be a waste of time."

"Goodnight Charly" she said and closed the door behind her.

She missed breakfast the next morning. She hated it waking up early. Her lifestyle was different to begin with. Most of the time she was just going to bed by the time these people were eating breakfast. Anyway, with much effort, she managed to show up at the booth by 9:30 am.

"I'm so sorry" she mumbled under her breath "but you were supposed to wake me up for breakfast, remember?" she said to Charles.

"It's alright. I wanted you to be rested. There is some coffee in the other room with some Danish pastries, if you want some." She went and poured herself a big cup of coffee.

"I'm gonna need a few of these, if I want to really wake up and switch my brain on" she thought to herself.

They were watching the doctors walking around, touching the instruments, asking endless questions and talking between each other in a language Isabelle had never heard. It was called medical language, Grant Hamilton told her. She felt so useless. She had no idea what all these people were talking about. She needed someone to fill her in, before she embarrassed, not only herself, but the whole company.

Charly felt her confusion and came to her rescue, as always, with a brilliant plan… he gave her a manual, where all the instruments were pictured, with detailed explanations about what are they used for and what material are they made from. You couldn´t go wrong with that book in your hand. As a backup, Grant was by her side and gave her a crash course in an hour. He took her around the rest of the show, and they checked out every stand and all the new product displays. They had lunch and by the early afternoon, Isabelle was talking to the numerous surgeons who'd gathered around her display table, explaining every single one of the instruments.

"I pray to God, they don't ask any questions out of the context and find out that in reality, I have no idea, what I'm talking about!" she said to Grant when they were alone.

"You're doing just fine, my darling!" he said and gave her a pat on her shoulder.

It was around 4 pm, when Nick called. Her heart sank and she stepped away from the stand.

"Hi" was all she managed to say.

"Hi sexy," Nick was all cheery "I'm on my way back to the city from Long Island and I am finished for today, so wondered if you could sneak away for an hour… I miss you."

"I don't know what time we're going to finish up here… but let me check and I'll call you back! I miss you too…sexy."

She put the phone down and went looking for Charly. She found him talking to Grant.

"Ah… excuse me, can you tell me, what time are we finishing today?"

"Around 5…5.30. Why?" Charles asked.

"I need to go back to my apartment" she lied "So I'll be gone for an hour or two, if you don't mind, but if it's a problem, I can do it tomorrow."

"No, it's ok. We're going to Sparks, the steak house, for dinner at 9 pm… Are you coming to join us?" "Sure" she said.

She called Nick and told him, she'd meet him at 5.30, but that she had to be back by the latest 8 o'clock.

The show closed at 5pm. She helped Charly put all the instruments back in the boxes and hurried back up to her room to get changed. She picked out a funky pair of jeans from 'Voyage Passion' and a pink and brown checked cashmere top from 'Les Copains'. The jeans had a pink velvet stripe at the bottom of the legs and the top was finished with a pink rabbit fur collar. She combed her hair and put on a rose velour cap. "Very British in pink", she thought, satisfied with the way she looked. She put on her high heeled boots and left the room.

There were lots of people in front of the Hotel, waiting for a taxi. She lit herself a cigarette and dialed Nick's number.

"No, better not," she thought "he'll think, I'm desperate. I'll wait."

It was only 5.20, 5 minutes later he was there. The top down on his car, and the music was loud. He was looking so handsome. He had taken off his jacket and tie and had unbuttoned the first two buttons of his shirt. He looked through the crowd and his lips turned into a smile the minute he saw her walking towards his car. She opened the door, sat down and looked at him.

"Hi babe," she said and put her hands around his neck, giving him a gentle kiss.

She tasted so good, he wanted to kiss her a hundred more times, or just simply never stop kissing her.

"Where do you wonna go?" he asked.

"I don't know, you're the New Yorker, not me. Somewhere only for a drink though, as I have to go for dinner with all my doctors and there's no way out of it. I need to be back here by 8 pm latest."

"O.K. No problem!"

They drove through the busy streets of Manhattan. He was a fast driver, sneaking in between the cars. It was dangerous, but exciting at the same time. Every time they stopped at a traffic light, he'd lean in to kiss her. She loved it. There was a big smile printed on her face, she was scared she'd not be able to remove it, ever.

He took her to a nice art deco bar, decorated all in white. The sofas, chairs, tables, walls… they were all white. They ordered a Cosmo and an apple martini, plus two kamikaze shots.

"Are you trying to get me drunk again?"

"Not really."

She was about to say something, but he stopped her with a long enthusiastic kiss.

"I'll take some more of that" she murmured and offered him more of her lips. They barely talked for the first half hour. It seemed like they really could read each other thoughts, looking at each other, without saying a word and kissing. Her lips were swollen and hurting, and his kisses were getting more and more demanding.

He was adorable, she thought, he never asked any questions, never tried to put his nose in her business and he seemed to like her just the way she was, without trying to change her, or judge her, like all the rest of the men she'd met in her life had tried to do. If she'd put in a request to God for a man, then he had sent her Nicholas Walters. She laughed at her thoughts.

"What's so funny?" he asked "I wonna laugh with you."

"I am not telling you that right now… probably one day though, if you deserve it."

He kissed her again. They had one more drink and left round 6.30 pm.

"Do you want me to show you around? Something, like a quick tour of Manhattan" he asked.

"Yes, please!"

He put the top down of his car, turned the music up loud and away they flew. He took her up 2nd avenue to 57th street and then they went all the way to 5th avenue. From there, they drove down, passing by the Rockefeller Plaza, then turned right and drove to 7th avenue, where he showed her Time Square. She wanted to scream with happiness. She wanted the whole world to know, how she felt. Instead, she looked at the young man sitting next to her and snuggled up to him. He felt her excitement and kissed her head. She melted inside. When he stopped his car in front of her hotel, she didn't want to say "Good bye", so she kissed him quick and jumped out of the car.

"I'll call you"…

Nick droved away, feeling a little confused…how could she be like that? First so warm and giving and then a minute later, so distant and cold. Did he do something wrong? He decided to ask her later… she said, she'd call him??What the hell was happening? It seemed Isabelle was the one wearing the pants here and he doing the chasing. He smiled.

"If that's what makes her happy, let her be the boss!"

Isabelle went to her room and called Charly to find out where they were meeting for dinner.

"8.30 pm, down in the bar" was the simple answer.

While sipping their martinis the doctors discussed the happenings of the day and they all praised Isabelle, for her skill in learning so quickly and about the effort she'd put into her assignment. She was smiling and nodding in agreement, but the words were only passing through her brain, without stopping. Her mind was still out there, on the streets of Manhattan with Nicholas Walters.

They took a limo to the restaurant. 'Sparks' was a well known steak house very traditional. Many celebrities have enjoyed the lobster and steak here, accompanied by the exclusive wines they offered.

Grant chose a bottle of 'Rothschild', an extraordinary French wine. Isabelle didn't want to sound snobby, so she stayed quiet, but she smiled with a delight, when she heard Grant's choice.

"That's a great bottle" she whispered.

Charles was sitting across the table looking at her.

"You know, we've been talking about you", he started "You've done a great job today and the doctors loved you. If you are interested, me and Grant were thinking about sending you on a training course. Here in New York. Two weeks. You'll learn about the material more deeply. We were thinking about arranging one week access for you to the operating room of one of the surgeons, so you can see live, what they are doing and how are they doing it. By that time, when you're done, you'll be able to explain our instruments, better than Grant himself. So, if all goes well with that and you keep up the dedication you've shown today, we would like to offer you the N.Y. area as our representative."

He fixed his eyes on her, followed by all the other pairs of eyes on the table.

She didn't just blush, she turned a bright red. She thought, there must be steam coming out of her ears.

"What's going on with all these people?" she asked herself "First Frank, now Charles with their crazy career offers! Have they all gone mad?"

"So, what do you think?" Charly's voice brought her back to the present.

"What do I think…?" she thought again, unable to bring even a word to her lips, "I think, I need a cigarette and I need to stop drinking…I've been drinking too much lately and I'm starting to imagine things."

But all she could say was she'd think about it.

They ordered dinner and kept discussing business. At one point Charly changed the subject and told a funny story about Grant, from their child hood. Grant had graduated from Harvard to become a doctor, as his father had been before him and his grandfather and his grandfather's grandfather, probably. Doctors are famous for being tight with their money. They never pay the restaurant or the bar bill, nor do they feel obliged to buy someone a drink. They are docs and that's how they are.

"What do they do with all their money then?" Isabelle asked.

"Giving it to the wives, so they can go shopping and stay out of the house!" Jay Luca said, and everyone laughed, besides Grant of course.

The evening turned out to be very pleasant and as Isabelle was the only woman at the table again, she enjoyed their admiration. She loved being the center of attention. She even forgot about Nick! Everything was great! Her future seemed to be getting very bright, if only one of these men kept his promises. There was one rule, she had never broken in her life to 'Never trust a man. Ever!' No matter what they do or say, men are not to be trusted. You can love them, hate them, play with them, but never trust them with your life, or your future. They might help you sometimes and you'll think. "Oh there's a good one!" Wrong!!! He was just in a good mood.

She was laughing at their jokes and the docs were giving her compliments, one after the other. And then suddenly something happened. She sat back in her chair and looked around. The restaurant was full with people. The waiters were running between the tables taking orders or bringing the food. Everybody was talking. She could hear the people on the next table, talking about their vacation and the women laughing… everybody seemed to be happy. She looked at the four men on her table. They were also smiling. All of them looking handsome, successful. Young, at the best time of their lives and she had the honor to be the center of their attention. She was sitting right there in the middle of everything. Charles Parrish and Grant Hamilton had just offered her a job anybody would kill for and then suddenly she got that sharp squeeze in her heart, her stomach was hurting and her throat was dry. There was something wrong and somewhere deep inside her mind, there was a question, looking desperately for an answer.

"What the hell am I doing here?" she asked herself and froze. She didn't want to be there. No! Not at all!

She wanted to be with Nicholas Walters in his one bedroom apartment, laying on his sofa, in his arms, feeling them wrapped around her. That simple. She didn't want this, she wanted that.

And then it hit her…

"I am in love."

She closed her eyes and prayed to God to help her. She knew love was the greatest power in this world. Anyone who has felt that power, has given themselves up to it. No one can defeat love. Not a single human being.

"I'm in love" she whispered to herself and got up from the table.

"Would you excuse me for a moment gentlemen," she said and walked away.

Chapter 12

Isabelle was walking nervously up and down the street with her cell phone in one hand and her cigarettes in the other. What was she supposed to do now? She could only think about one thing, to call Nick and tell him about how she felt... but that wasn't what women normally do, was it? She had never been in love before, so she didn't know how to manage things right in a situation like this. She'd been with lots of men, had dated most of them and always got what she wanted from them, but that was a different thing. It wasn't love. It was a game of love for her, and she was the best player. She knew the rules and she was always in control. So, what was she supposed to do now? She had no clue. It wouldn't be a good idea to go back in the restaurant and share her thoughts with the doctors. She could call her sister, that could work! She dialed the number.

Her sister lived in Orlando, Florida. She was younger than Isabelle, but already married and had a beautiful baby. She had married as a virgin, so she must've been in love with her husband and she still was, according to her own words. Sadly, Isabelle never listened to her sister's stories. They sounded always so boring.

Silvia answered the phone with a sleepy voice.

"What's happening sis? I'm in bed by the way!"

"I know, I know, but I need you sis."

Silvia set up in her bed. For being the younger one, life had worked out differently. Normally, it was always Isabelle making a mess and getting into trouble and Silvia was always there to help her!!A sister to dream about! Silvia was always there no matter what... always listening and never judging her big sister.

"What kind of trouble are you in this time?" she asked with a worried voice.

"I'm in love" Isabelle answered.

"Oh for God's sake! It's eleven in the evening. I have to work tomorrow. Have you been drinking!?" she said and put the phone down.

Isabelle was staring at the phone in her hand in disbelieve. Speechless! She pressed the redial button, but Silvia had turned her phone off. She deserved it. How many times has she cried down the phone and claimed that she was in love with someone and then a few days later couldn't even remember his name. No wonder Silvia wasn't taking her seriously. Isabelle didn't know what love was. Not until today!

She smoked her cigarette and decided to get back inside the restaurant.

"Where were you?" Charly said "We thought you'd left us."

"Almost" she answered, and they all laughed, assuming she was joking. If they only knew...if they could read her mind, they wouldn't be laughing.

They were working on the third bottle of wine and Isabelle was helping with great enthusiasm, since she'd come back from her cigarette break.

"The alcohol will make me forget about all that crap" she thought "I'll get tired, go to bed early tonight and have a fresh and bright start tomorrow morning."

That was the plan, and she was determined to follow it. She felt better, she was getting the control back again.

Charly paid the bill and the group returned to the hotel. They all had one last drink at the bar. Isabelle excused herself and wished everybody a good night. She went back to her room, turned the TV on, laid on the couch…and then lost all the control she thought she'd regained. Like in a trance she took her cell out of her purse and dialed Nick's number.

"Hi, I've been thinking about you" he'd obviously seen her number on the screen.

"How was your evening?"

"Great. Thanks for asking. I…" she stuttered "I was thinking about you too. I need to talk to you but I don't know how to begin."

The wine had gone straight to her head. She felt like she wasn't laying on the couch anymore, but swimming.

On the other end of the line, Nick went silent for a long moment.

"What's wrong?" he asked, his voice tight. "Did I do something wrong today to upset you?…If I did, I'm sorry. Listen, I didn't mean to. I…" He stopped talking. He didn't know what to tell her. He was thinking about the way she'd left earlier. Given him a quick insignificant kiss, with a brief "I'll call you". His heart sank. Maybe he had been too pushy and had scared her away and now it was too late. If she would only give him another chance.

"It's not you babe," her voice was quiet "It's me."

That was what they always say, he thought. The next thing she'd be telling him that he was a great guy, and he deserved better than her. But he didn't want better, he wanted her.

"I've been thinking about you most of the evening" she said, "and I have to tell you that, 'coz, I can't keep it to myself any longer."

"What is it honey?" his voice was smooth.

"I…I'm falling in love with you."

There was a heavy silence. She could hear him breathing.

"Are you still there?" she asked.

"Yes" was the only word he said.

"I need to see you. Can I come over to your place?"

"I'll tell the doorman you're coming and will leave the door open."

She put the phone down and left the room. Her heart was racing. She couldn't think. She didn't know whether what she was doing was right or wrong and she didn't care. All she knew was that she wanted to kiss him and be in his arms. She was in love.

She opened the door to his apartment. It was dark. The lights were off. It took her a few minutes to adjust her eyes to the darkness and then she saw him, laying on the couch, looking at her. She sat next to him. They were both looking at each other in silence. He touched her hair, her face. Her skin felt so good, so soft. The scent of her perfume filled the room. She leaned towards him and gave him a soft, insecure kiss, barely touching his lips. There was a still silence in the room except she could hear him breathing and he could hear her. The moment was magical. Just the two of them, like the world around them didn't exist. She kissed him again and he pulled her to him, locking his arms around her. He could feel her breasts against his chest, he could count her heart beats. She didn't know what she wanted, but he did, and he knew how to give it to her. He wanted her so much, he wanted to love every inch of her. He wanted to give her everything and please her in every possible way. He had to watch himself. He wanted to be gentle and slow, so he had to control himself and the hurricane inside him. It was difficult, it gained strength with every touch, every kiss. The desire was becoming furious and almost out of control, threatening to sweep them both away.

"I couldn't stop thinking about you" she whispered, her eyes gazing at him with a thousand stars in them.

"I couldn't stop thinking about you either" he pressed his body against her. She was caressing his chest gently.

"I need you…" the words caught in her throat. His skin was hot, melting under her fingertips.

He couldn't control himself anymore either. He needed her. Her hands left a trail of shimmering sensations across his skin. He couldn't wait any longer. He took her in his arms, carried her to his bedroom and put her gently on his bed.

"Don't move" he said, as he slowly undressed her. She was laying there looking up at him, admiringly and he was looking down at her, admiring her beauty.

They made passionate love that night. It felt again, as if they were one. They reached their high point together and she felt her tears rolling down her face.

"What's wrong with me?" she thought "I'm behaving like I'm a virgin or back at high school."

She turned around, trying to hide her tears from him, but he'd already seen them. He felt the same way, but men were not allowed to cry…so he just held her tight in his arms, until they both felt asleep, without saying a word.

Words were not necessary at that moment. What they needed to know, they knew in their hearts.

It was 8 o'clock on Sunday morning, when she opened her eyes.

"Oh my God, I'm late." she cried out.

She turned around and saw him laying next to her, still asleep. She touched his forehead gently with her lips and ran into the bathroom for a quick shower. She got dressed in the living room, because she didn't want to wake him up. She was ready to leave, when he came from behind her and pulled her in his arms.

"Are you trying to run away from me?" he kissed her on her neck, making her shiver. "No, no, it doesn't work this way, my angel! You can't run away from me anymore. I need you in my life."

She turned around, put her arms around his neck and their eyes met.

"I'm not running away, I promise. I have to be back in the showroom at 9 am, so I'm late. I'll see you later tonight, maybe?" she looked at him with hope.

"I'll leave the door open. Maybe I'll come to see you this afternoon…which floor is the show on?"

"14th"… she had to go, so she kissed him one last time and left.

Chapter 13

Isabelle found Charly and Grant at the stand. She was late again, but at least she was half an hour earlier than yesterday! Only 9 am not 9:30! She grabbed herself a cup of coffee and joined the two men.

"Good morning, gentlemen!" she said with a bright smile, all glowing.

"Did you just come down from Heaven, or you did you spend the night with an angel? You are all joy and happiness!"

"I think it was the second one" she smiled conspiratorially.

They went back to work and the conversation was brought back to medical instruments, plastic surgery and doctors. She was talking to everyone, explaining patiently, why Parrish instruments were the best on the market at the moment etc. but she felt as if she could fly.

Her sister called her later that afternoon.

"Are you still in love or is it over already?"

"It's different this time, I know it for sure."

"But that's what you always say sis, until two days later!"

"No really, totally different. Can I please tell you the whole story ," Isabelle insisted "His name is Nicholas Walters, and he is from NY…"

"Sis, I love you and I don't want you to be mad with me, but I don't want to hear the story. Let's talk about him in a week, if he still exists."

That sounded quite fair to Isabelle, so they agreed on that.

Silvia was in the real estate business in Florida. She was very hard working and down to earth, the exact opposite of her sister, who still believed in Santa Claus and was a total dream head. That's why they completed each other.

The day passed so quickly and the Medical Show came to it's close. By the time they had taken down the stand and put everything away in boxes, it was 7.30pm. She had talked briefly to Nick, but she knew she wouldn't be able to see him tonight. Charles and Grant had already warned her that they were all going for dinner later. It was their last night in the city, the next morning they would all be going back to Boston.

She got changed into a pair of black trousers and a black cashmere combo. She had no idea where they were going, so she decided to play it safe. To her surprise, they ended up in 'Le Colonial' on 57th street. She loved that place.

A great kitchen, a cross between French and Vietnamese cuisine, a very exotic combination. After dinner, they all went to the bar in the Peninsula Hotel. The night went by as quickly as the day. Time was flying. Isabelle couldn't wait to get back to her room and call Nick.

She'd told him about her day and about the offer Charles had made her at dinner, the night before. She'd never revealed anything about herself to the other guys she'd dated. She never told anybody, anything about herself, in general. Normally she'd be accused of being so secretive, but with him, the words just poured out of her and she could tell him everything. That was an amazing new feeling for her. She was used to sharing her ups and downs, her problems and joys, only with Silvia, but of course it wasn't the same. It felt like he was a part of her and not just there next to her.

"Are you coming over tonight?" Nick asked her.

She was so tired and to be honest she hadn't had much sleep the whole of the last week.

"I'm going to bed straight away honey. Sorry, but I'm too tired to move."

"Are you working tomorrow? I mean, are you working in the club?" he asked.

"Oh yes! So, I'll be free during the day and working at night time again… The opposite to you, ha!… I'm sure we'll find a way to see each other anyway! I miss you!" she whispered.

"So when is your day off? You don't work every day, all the time, do you?"

"No!" she laughed, "I have Friday and Saturday off and work from Sunday to Thursday. What about you?"

"I'm in the office from Monday to Saturday and only have Sunday off. I work a lot, and hard… from 7 am 'til 9 pm."

"What?" she almost choked on her water." Are you a workaholic or something?

She usually worked between 4 and 6 hours a day, but him?! It didn't sound right. She really wasn't into workaholics, people who live to work and to whom their career means their life. She liked successful people and knew success needed hard work, but 15 hours a day, 6 days a week…her heart sank. He won't have any time for her.

"No, no, it's not as bad as it sounds. I finish at 4 pm on Fridays and go to the office only for a couple of hours on Saturdays." He could feel her relief, after he explained that to her. They talked a little longer and then she went to bed.

The next time she saw Nick was on the Thursday of the following week but they had been talking regularly on the phone. She'd got used to calling him every night after work on her way home. If she hadn't called him by 4.30 am he would call her to make sure she was all right. He woke her up every day at 12 am and sent her tons of messages throughout the day. She was the happiest girl in the world.

He called on Thursday and invited her for a drink before she went to work.

They met at 'Merchants', a cigar bar on the corner of 61st street and 1st avenue. He couldn't keep his hands off her and she couldn't keep her lips off his.

"Will you go out with me on Saturday?" he asked her.

"What about Friday?" she shot back.

"Oh, yes, I mean Friday! Holy Shit, that's tomorrow!! So, will you go out with me on Friday and Saturday? I would love to take you out for a nice meal!"

"Are you asking me out on a date, Mr. Walters?" she stopped kissing him and asked playfully.

They both laughed. They had never actually been out on a date yet.

"Yes Madame, I am indeed!"

"I'll see what I can do!" she said and rolled her eyes "I need to check with my secretary first."

"…and when you're checking with her for Friday, make sure you check also for Saturday!"

She didn't want to leave him and go to work, but she had to… she had to go back to reality, where money ruled the world and kisses and love came second.

The next couple of weeks went like in a dream. Isabelle was working, four days a week and spending every weekend with Nick in his place. They went out for dinners on Fridays, clubbing on Saturdays and chilling on the sofa on Sundays.

Then she stopped working on Sundays, after a small incident she had at the club…

They'd spent Friday and Saturday together and on the Sunday he'd taken her for a brunch on the west side and afterwards they'd gone to the National History Museum. They had such a great time. He showed her the dinosaurs. They went to see the forgotten city of Petra. Then later on, they made love, laid on the sofa and watched a movie. Nick ordered takeout and they ate at home. She left for work at 8 pm. She went to the club, got changed and went to the bar and ordered a strong double martini.

"This doesn't feel right" she thought. "Being here when Nick is at work is ok, but right now, after all we did today, I had to leave my man at home alone and come and dance here for another one. Fuck no!"

She was getting more and more upset by the minute.

"Nice to see you again" she heard April's voice. "Where have you been all this time?"

Isabelle was pleased to see her friend.

"I am going back to Scotland tomorrow. I've changed my flight. Need to go home hun, I miss my baby boy so much."

April had a six year old son, who was staying with her boyfriend back at home.

"I'll miss you" Isabelle said.

"Babe, you're spending all your time with Mr. Walters. You have Frank and Nick and I'm here all alone. I am tired of NY. I miss my home, my friends, my boyfriend and my wee boy."

She was right, Isabelle thought. April was lonely. Before they were together all the time and lately, they barely saw each other. Only at work or they talked on the phone, but that was not the same. April had accepted the fact that Isabelle was in love, and nothing could change that, but she would miss her friend. She gave her a hug.

"I just came to empty my locker and say good bye to you, Jordan! You have my number in Scotland, haven't you?"

Isabelle had tears in her eyes. April was really annoying sometimes but she loved her. They were best friends after all. She didn't want her to leave.

"Listen babe, you can call me any time, you know I'm always there for you. Come and see me in London, when you are back in Europe, and I'll come to see you in Spain." She gave her a kiss on the cheek. "My flight is tomorrow morning, so I have to go now. Love you" and that was it, she was gone.

Another double martini was called for.

"This is even worse" she thought "First I leave my man alone at home and now my best friend leaves me alone in here."

She finished her drink and went to talk to the manager. Half an hour later, she was standing in front of Nick's apartment, trying to unlock the door with the key he'd given her. He was asleep on the couch and the TV was still on. She stopped in the middle of the room, looking at him, her eyes full of tears. He felt someone was watching him and opened his eyes. He saw her. Jumped off the sofa and ran to her. She was in such a mess. His heart started to beat faster and faster and his face showed his fear.

"What happened to you honey? Are you all right? God, why are you crying babe?"

It was breaking his heart to see her like this. He took her in his arms and stroked her hair, trying to make her feel safe.

"Everything will be alright. You'll see, whatever's happened will go away. I'm here for you darling. Please don't cry!" She held him tighter.

"I've missed you so much…I was thinking about you being here alone…and I wanted to hold you so much… and then April left for good…and I was feeling so lonely. I just couldn't stay there any longer."

And she never worked on a Sunday again.

Chapter 14

Time was passing quickly. It seemed Isabelle and Nick were living in their own world, without letting anybody else in it. She was happy like never before and he was the man she'd been looking for.

"I'm going to London next week" she said.

She didn't really wanted to leave him, but it was too late to change her mind. She had promised Frank, weeks ago, the tickets were paid, the hotel was booked, and she could use the 5000 dollars.

"Why are you going to London?" He was surprised. "You never told me about it."

"I forgot. I'm sorry. It'll only be for a week. I need to take care of things over there and I want to go and check on my dad and my house in Spain. Make sure everything is as I left it and all the bills are paid."

She didn't even look at him while she was talking. She hated lying to him, but she was scared to tell him the truth too. Besides, last time she spoke to Frank, they agreed to go to Mallorca for two days, so it wasn't all a lie. She was actually telling the truth, just leaving out some small unimportant details… like Frank traveling with her and that she was getting 5000 dollars. Shit, that didn't sound good. He'll never believe the real story behind the whole arrangement anyway so, forget it!

Nick wasn't very happy, but there wasn't a lot he could do about it.

The flight to London was leaving at 8 am from J.F.K. International airport. Frank and Isabelle were both sitting in MacDonald's at Terminal 2 trying to cure the hangover by eating a big fat Big Mac.

They'd not gone to bed the night before. Isabelle had been working in the club and Frank had gone out for dinner with friends. Around 1 am, on his way back to the apartment he'd decided to check on some last minute details about the trip with Isabelle and stopped by to see her. The ten minutes, he'd meant to spend, turned into three hours, two bottles of red wine and couple of kamikaze shots. The limo was coming to pick them up at 5.30 am, so they had just enough time for a quick shower before they had to go.

They were still tipsy when they arrived at the airport, so Isabelle suggested, before they got into trouble with security, that they should eat something to help them sober up a bit. She couldn't wait to sit in her seat and close her eyes.

"I'll be sleeping all the way to London, so please don't wake me up for any reason. I don't want to eat or drink anything anymore" she said.

"Uh huh" he groaned.

The next time she opened her eyes, the captain of the flight was welcoming his passengers to Heathrow international airport. "Are we here?" She rubbed her eyes and looked around only to find Frank still snoring in the seat next to hers.

"Wake up, we're here now!" she was getting excited.

She looked out of the small window. It wasn't Spain, but it was Europe!! It felt like home to her, especially after being away in the US for more than three months. She had missed her old world.

Frank opened his eyes and the first thing he felt was a severe headache.

"Damn, remind me never to order any alcohol when you're around. You're a very bad influence, Miss Lucardi." They both laughed.

It took them about an hour and a half before they arrived at their hotel. Frank's secretary had booked the Sheraton Park Tower for them. The hotel was perfectly situated and had one of the best casinos in town. Two blocks away from Bond Street, a five minute walk from Harrods and five minutes away from the famous shops on Sloan Street.

They checked in and arranged to meet back at the reception in an hour.

Isabelle couldn't wait to take a long hot shower. Last night had been pretty hard, but at least they'd had some sleep on the plane.

First things first! She turned her cell phone on. Sent a message to Nick, but after a minute of hesitation, she decided, she needed to hear his voice too.

It was 9 pm in London that meant it had to be 4 pm in New York. Nick had to be in his office. She left the phone ringing 'til the mail box kicked in.

"I miss you" she whispered and blew him an air kiss.

She got ready and went to meet with Frank and his friends.

They were already waiting for her. Frank introduced her to Steven and Kelly, both from New York. Steven was on the board of directors of Frank's Company, and Kelly was the finance supervisor. They seemed to be really nice people and both appeared very professional.

It was getting late, so they decided to get something to eat in the hotel. Luckily, the casino had a small restaurant attached to it, offering a Mediterranean kitchen with a strong Arabic accent.

London was the most popular and beloved get away for the people from the Gulf Countries. It was hundreds of years ago when Britain had tried to colonize the Arabic world, it seemed now that the Arabs were doing the same to London.

Especially the people from Dubai. They had made the old British capital their second home town.

Steven, who was a frequent visitor to London and usually stayed in the Sheraton Park Tower, had a membership card for the casino. He put the rest of the group on the guest list, except Isabelle. She decided to use the situation and apply for one of her own. It worked! She could pick up her own membership card in twenty four hours.

It turned to be a great night! Frank gave her two hundred pounds worth of tokens and she and Kelly hit the roulette tables after dinner. They were doing quite well. The guys were playing Black Jack… Isabelle loved casinos…and high bets. The adrenaline kick was similar to the one she had after taking a few lines of cocaine.

"Let's put everything on black or red" she said "then we can relax, go to the bar and have a drink.

Kelly was kind of skeptical. She was a lot more conservative with her decisions, but it was Isabelle's game.

"Do what you want to do!"

Isabelle had no option but to like that girl. That seemed to be her favorite phrase… 'do what you want to do'. She laughed and put everything on red.

The ball rolled around and fell on thirty six, red.

"We won!" she screamed out and everyone turned in her direction.

They were the proud owners of eight hundred and fifty pounds.

"Shall we play some more?" she turned to Kelly.

"Do what you want to do!"

"Listen, we'll do it like this…you take four hundred pounds and don't give it to me, no matter what I say. I play the rest.

Whatever I win, we share it."

"It's a deal!"

Kelly took the tokens and went to the bar, while Isabelle went back to her game. Half an hour later, she saw Isabelle walking her way, with a huge smile on her face, her eyes glittering and her hands full with tokens.

"You did it again girl!"

"It's got to be my lucky night!" she couldn't hide her excitement. "Can you believe this? A thousand pounds each!

Sterling! You owe me a drink, girl!"

"Have you seen Frank and Steve?" Kelly asked.

"I think I saw them in the back of the room, playing baccarat." Isabelle said.

Her phone rang. It had to be Nick.

"Hello."

"Hey honey, I'm sorry, I missed your call earlier, I was in a meeting. Anyway, how was your flight?"

"Perfect! Slept through most of it…I miss you honey… wish you were here with me…I went out for dinner with my friend Kelly, and we're having a drink at the hotel bar…the last one, I promise!"

Kelly gave her a puzzled look.

"I really miss you babe" Isabelle couldn't suppress a smile

"Just be good and don't kiss any other girls, while I am away!"

"Don´t be stupid! Why would I do that?"

"Because you're a man!" Oops, that was a bit too sharp, she thought. "I'm only joking with you! I know you'd never do anything to hurt me…I trust you honey."

She was so close to telling him that she loved him, but she bit her lip. Not yet! When she's back in New York! She needed to look into his eyes when she tells him that. The first time she told him, she wanted to do it right.

"Sending you a thousand kisses babe. I'll try to call you before I go to bed."

She looked at Kelly and blushed.

"Was that your boyfriend?"

"No, my brother" Isabelle laughed "of course it was my boyfriend, Nick."

"Where's he from?"

"Upstate New York, but he lives in Midtown Manhattan now…and I'm so in love with him…it seems almost unreal."

"How long have you been together?" Kelly seemed to be very curious.

"A month, a bit over a month probably!"

"It's normal to feel like that then. Give it some more time and things will cool down."

Isabelle wanted to slap her, right across her grinning face.

"I don't want things to cool down! I'm not complaining, I like them the way they are and don't want them to change!"

"I know, honey, but that's the way the game of love normally works!"

"Hey, this is not a game…we are not playing…or at least I'm not…" Isabelle whispered.

She looked at her tokens, took a sip of her drink, but all of her ecstatic mood from before had gone. The sun wasn't shining anymore and the sky was covered in dark clouds.

"I'm tired from the flight." She tried to change the conversation. "Best thing I need right now is a good night sleep." Kelly felt her mood change and tried to cheer her up.

"Don't worry darling. I didn't mean that Nick will stop loving you or like you less…I only meant the butterflies in your stomach will fly away. Only the first kiss is called 'The First Kiss', but it doesn't make it the best one, does it?!"

"You're right…I'm not worried, just tired. I´ll see you mañana!"

She went to find the men, wished them good night and went to her room. Sleep didn't come easy though, Kelly's words were still causing chaos in her mind.

What if it was just a game for Nick?

She'd done the same thing to other men, so many times.

They had meant what they were saying but for her it had been nothing but a game…she thought they knew that! Most of them didn't! How could she know if Nick was playing her now, or if he was real?

"Only time will tell!"

Chapter 15

The next morning, she woke up at 6 am. She went down to the breakfast room to find Frank, sitting in front of a coffee pot, with a newspaper in his hands.

"Good morning! Up early today!"

"Must be the time change, but I feel great...not tired at all. So, what's the plan for today, Sir?"

"Steven and I are having a few meetings before noon and Kelly is going to our English office to check on some paperwork."

"So, I have the half of the day for myself!" Isabelle exclaimed delightedly.

"Go shopping!" Frank suggested" I've heard you won a bit of cash last night! And what about April? I thought you wanted to meet up with her!"

She had totally forgotten about April! And even worse, she'd left her number behind in New York in her other cell. Holy shit! Anyway she didn't want to think about that right now.

Emma! She would call Emma! Her childhood friend, who'd moved to London a year and a half ago.

"What time do you think, you'll be done with your meetings?"

"No idea, but it won't be before 1pm. I'll call you as soon as we finish."

"That's cool with me!"

They had breakfast together and Frank left to meet with Steven and Kelly, leaving Isabelle by herself at the table with the newspaper.

It was too early to call anyone. It was the middle of the night in New York and too early in the morning in London. Emma, for sure, would not be awake before 10 am.

Emma was the exact description of what you call a lady of leisure and very high maintenance. She'd been married to a Spanish property dealer, got divorced and moved to London.

Last year, Emma had dated an Arab sheikh, or something similar, an American businessman who had chosen England for his second home. Isabelle had no idea who was she dating now, but one thing was sure, he was filthy rich.

She decided to go out for a walk. Knightsbridge was a good area to wander around.

The air was fresh as always in England, so she got dressed up warm and left the hotel, not forgetting to take a small umbrella in her handbag… best to be prepared, you never knew if it was going to start raining in London!

She wondered through the shops around the hotel, but she didn't see anything she really liked.

Emma finally answered her phone after 11 am. They arranged to meet at the Tea Room in the Four Seasons Hotel.

It was nice to see her friend again. She hadn't seen her since the summer, when she'd come to Mallorca for a week or so. She hadn't changed a bit!

Emma was still living in her own dream world. She was always in a good mood, always smiling, very well spoken and with fine manners.

"She and Charles Parrish would've made a great couple" thought Isabelle.

They talked for an hour, trying to catch up on the latest happenings, when Frank called.

"I'm starving!" he groaned.

Isabelle gave him the address and he showed up ten minutes later. Then they all went to a small Italian bistro somewhere around Sloane Street.

Frank was totally blown away by Emma, who was flirting with him nonstop.

They went to check out the boutiques later and Isabelle got lost in Louis Vuitton.

"I can't believe my eyes!" she said, pointing to one of the suitcases where you hang your shirts without folding them. "I've been looking for one of those everywhere!"

"What's so special about it?" Frank asked.

"You see, they've been making that type of case for years, but not in this particular style. And I have the medium size roller in the exact same style. It's called Damiere!" she gently touched the check print on the piece she was admiring. "The lady from Louis Vuitton in NY, told me it would cost me one thousand, five hundred dollars and I had to wait six months for a special order." "And they have it here" Emma clapped her hands.

Isabelle was all over the suitcase, not letting it out of her grip.

"Nine hundred, forty five pounds!" Frank was shocked "Are you out of your mind? Go get yourself a nice case from Tumi. It will cost you one third of this price."

"It's not about the price" Emma corrected him "it's about image and style."

Isabelle couldn't think of a better way to spend the money she'd won the night before. She paid and asked for it to be sent to her hotel.

It was a very successful day, after all!

Frank was so impressed with Emma, so he invited her to join them for dinner. Steven had made a reservation in 'San Lorenzo', said to be the best Italian restaurant in town.

Even Princess Diana had been counted as one of his guests before her tragic death. Numerous Formula One drivers and super models, movie stars etc. Exactly the perfect ambience for Emma Garcia.

After a great night, Frank and Isabelle were on their way to Heathrow again. They were going to Palma de Mallorca for two days. Two days and one night exactly. The return flight was late in the evening of the following day.

Isabelle was busy talking on the phone to her dad and Frank was staring out of the taxi window.

It was raining. Grey and cold weather. If it wasn't for the bad weather London would be the best city in the world.

It was the financial capital of Europe, same as NY in the USA, but with a lot more traditions and history behind it. Frank was originally born in England, but his parents had emigrated to America. That was how he ended up having two passports, British and American. He always said that one day he would move back to England, but as yet he had only moved from California to Florida.

Chapter 16

"You will love it!" Isabelle said.

He had no idea what was she talking about.

"You will fall in love with the island. I promise you… That's what happened to me the first time, I saw it!"

Isabelle had grown up in Barcelona. Her parents had a summer house in the Costa Brava, so that's where they spent the summers. Until they decided to get divorced. Her father moved to Mallorca and her mom stayed in Barcelona. The first time Isabelle had seen the island was on her sixteenth birthday. She didn't know then, that one day it would become her home.

Mallorca was the biggest of the four Balearic Islands. Palma, the capital city, had almost half a million people living in it.

Their flight landed at 11.30 am. Her dad, Carlos, was there to pick them up. Carlos and Frank knew each other from London. It was Isabelle who had met Frank first, through a mutual friend three years ago. Two years ago, when she was in England with her dad, they met again.

Frank had invited them both for dinner and they'd always stayed in touch.

Carlos was happy to see them both.

He loved Isabelle. She was his only daughter. Silvia, her sister, was her mom's second husband's child.

Carlos was sixty three years old and as an enthusiastic golfer, was still in a good shape. He'd been happily living on the island for more than twenty years. But his happiest moment was when his daughter decided to move there 7 years ago. He gave her a big hug and shook hands with Frank.

"Nice to see you again, how was the flight?"

"Like an Easy Jet flight" Isabelle said, and they all laughed.

First stop was Isabelle's house, so they could take a shower and get rid of their luggage. Frank wanted to stop in a hotel, but Isabelle wouldn't hear of it. She insisted that he stayed in her guest room.

It was a beautiful, brand new, three bedroom penthouse, overlooking the sea. All the floors were white marble, as were the bathrooms. The kitchen had granite tops and was furnished with the latest top end appliances. Frank was impressed. He knew she had expensive tastes, but hadn't expected exactly that.

"This place is amazing" he said.

"Yeah, I know!"

He could see the pride in her eyes.

"There is only a tiny little problem with it… I'm not sure I can afford it… But what's done is done! It took many sacrifices, but now it's mine and I love it. And anyway, the bank financed only sixty percent of it, so I don't have a very high mortgage to pay." "Well done blondie" Frank teased her.

She went out on the terrace. It was a nice autumn day in Mallorca, around sixteen degrees, the sun was shining, and she could feel the warm breeze. She loved it here. It was her paradise…it had everything, she needed…except Nick! Oh my God she had forgotten to call him. She took her phone and dialed the number.

"Hey honey," His sleepy voice came through "Good morning my angel."

"Did I wake you up? So sorry babe, I didn't think about the time difference."

She checked her watch. 12.30am, it had to be 6.30 am in NY. "I miss you so much" he whispered "I need to hold you in my arms, kiss your lips, smell your skin, I need to be with you…"

"I miss you too babe, I'm back in three days…I'm in Mallorca

now and it's beautiful here, wish you were here with me!"

"Next time for sure."

She gave him an air kiss and let him have some more sleep.

She loved that man so much… What an amazing feeling that was. It wasn't about taking from him, it was all about giving to him, pleasing him and making him happy every day. Love was great and she loved it!

They went to Puerto Portals for lunch.

Portals was said to be one of the most expensive and prestigious ports, leaving Miami and Puerto Banus, as well as the one in Monte Carlo, behind.

She looked around and tried to absorb the luxury with every one of her senses. It felt and smelled like home…it was home for her.

They had a plate of freshly caught langoustines grilled in garlic butter and a typical Spanish dish for three, called Paella Marsico.

The food was excellent. After lunch, Isabelle took Frank for a walk around. They wandered between the yachts, while she tried to explain which boat belonged to which celebrity. They stopped for a café con leche in 'Cappuccino' and checked out the boutiques. There was something for everyone. The port definitely had its own flare. It was like a fantasy world.

The day came and left. They went to Palma for the evening. Frank was really very impressed with the architecture of the city. It is thousands of years old and still so amazing.

They checked out the old town, La Llonja, ate some tapas and drank Albariño, a light Spanish white wine. Isabelle met a couple of friends, and they all went for a glass of champagne in the Golden Door, a fashionable bar in the old town.

"You were right…I'm falling in love with it! I love it! You are a lucky girl, señorita Lucardi, for living here!"

Carlos had joined them, and Frank had told him already about his intention to hire Isabelle to work for him. His plan was to send her on a training program and after that, transfer her to London, where she would be looking for new clients and taking care of the old ones.

Isabelle had told Carlos briefly about Nick, but he didn't know the whole story, as they hadn't had enough time yet.

It was hard to believe they were leaving again tomorrow to go back to the Jungle…but Nick was there, in the Jungle…

"But one day" she thought "One day we'll be together forever and one day, after I show him this Paradise, he'll fall in love with it as well and we'll be living here together, happily ever after!"

She smiled and sat back in her chair. It was time to go, they would be flying back to London tomorrow evening.

Isabelle and Frank arrived back in the Sheraton Park tower, later in the evening that next day. The trip had been good for both. Relaxing and had recharged their batteries. It was time to go back to NY.

Their flight was leaving on Thursday afternoon.

Chapter 17

"Do you want me to pick you up from the airport?" Nick asked her.

"Oh, no don't worry…" She panicked. " I'll jump in a taxi, it's easier. And I need to go home first anyway…but I will see you straight after that!"

"You'd better! I've made arrangements for dinner… you'll love it!"

"Hmm, are you taking me somewhere romantic?…I'd rather have a delivery and eat dinner in bed."

"That's on the program for lunch tomorrow…and maybe dinner as well, we'll see! Tonight though, I'm taking you out. Do you want me to pick you up from yours or should I send a car for you?"

"As you want babe. I need to go now."

It was late in the afternoon when Isabelle and Frank arrived back at One Sutton Place. It was a chilly day in New York. She looked out of the window. There was a traffic jam on the Queensboro Bridge. It was getting dark, so she could see the city was dressed up in it's millions of dazzling lights…and she was there too… a small light in a big town. She drifted away with her thoughts… "How about if we could live between New York and Mallorca?" she wondered. That would be like living a dream. Spending the summers in Spain and the winters in New York. Summer in Paradise and Christmas in the Big Apple…"

"What's your plan for tonight?" Frank brought her back from her daydreaming.

"I'm going to work" She answered promptly.

"Are you crazy? Aren't you tired from the flight?"

"No, I slept on the plane."

She wasn't sure if she wanted to tell Frank about Nick yet. She was scared Frank might suggest that she should move in with Nick, and she didn't want to take that step just yet. Besides, Nick hadn't mentioned anything of the sort himself, so best to keep quiet about it for the moment.

"If you change your mind, I'm meeting Steve and Kelly later. You won't want to miss this. We have a table at 'Daniel'. Steve booked it three weeks ago."

He disappeared in his room.

That was a good try on Frank's part. She could so easily be manipulated sometimes. Promise her a good bottle of wine and a gourmet kitchen and she'd be right there! Not this time though!

"I really need to go to work…need to make some money!" "I just gave you a check for five thousand dollars last week!" "Last week! You said it! Now we're in this week!" She laughed.

The car was coming to pick her up at 8 pm. Frank had already gone to meet his friends, so she could take all the time she wanted to get ready. She wanted everything to be perfect tonight. She took a long bath, styled her hair, did her make up. She decided on a pair of beige, tight, low cut leather pants and a crème colored cashmere top. It was nice, elegant, yet still looked sexy on her. She didn't want to put on a dress, incase it looked too formal. The brown high heels with the same color handbag went perfectly together. She had bought them at Salvatore Ferragamo and loved them. They could make every outfit look special. She looked in the mirror and was completely satisfied with what she saw.

"Show time!" she said out loud smiling and left for the car.

Chapter 18

He was waiting for her in his apartment. It had been a week now, since the last time he'd seen her. He'd only known her for a month and a half but it felt to him as if he'd known her forever. She was different from the other girls he'd dated, and he fallen for her difference. He could see her in his future. If he closed his eyes and imagined his life five years from now, she was there… in the picture in his head. No one else had been there before. Sometimes he would see a silhouette but now that silhouette had Isabelle's face.

At that moment Isabelle arrived, or rather, stormed into his apartment and thrown herself into his arms. He wasn't even given the chance to say "Hello"!

"That's what I love about her" he thought. "Her spontaneous character…it came so naturally to her."

She was kissing him furious, with a fiery passion that could burn them both.

"I've missed you." She murmured.

"I was counting the days!" he added.

He had to get the control of the situation now though. They had to try to put the stops on this burning desire for the moment...he had plans for the night, and they had a limo waiting for them downstairs.

"Can we put a hold on this for later?" he whispered in her ear. "No" she said and her kisses became even more demanding.

She had waited so long for him to make love to her. Her arms were around his neck and her body arched up against his. He could feel her breasts against his chest while she bit on his lips, her body pressing against the hardness of his manhood.

He was going to lose this fight, he thought but just at that moment someone rang the doorbell.

It was enough to shake them both up and bring them back to reality. He pulled her to her feet and lifted her into his arms.

"We have to go" he said and gave her a kiss on her nose.

Nick took her to a very chic, posh restaurant downtown called Acappella! It seemed he'd been there a few times, as all the waiters knew him. They had dinner and drank two bottles of Brunello di Montalcino 97.

Towards the end of the dinner, Nick pulled something from his pocket to give to her.

"Take it" he said.

"What is it?" she asked.

"It's an ecstasy!"

"I don't do ecstasy...I drink, smoke and do cocaine, especially when I'm at work, but I don't do pills."

"Trust me!" he said and put it in her hand.

"Cheers!" she said and swallowed it with a sip of wine.

Later that evening they met up with some of Nick's friends. Isabelle was high on the pill and she was stuck to Nick, not letting go of his hand, not even for a second.

They were in a night club, somewhere in Manhattan. She had no idea where, exactly. Everything was swimming around her. She looked at him and pressed herself against his body. His arms locked around her.

"I love you." she said, her body quivering.

He pulled her tighter and started kissing her gently.

"I love you too honey…I love you too."

He took her hand, and they fled the club, jumped into the limo and asked the driver to take them home.

Nick was feeling high as hell. He looked at Isabelle. Fuck, she was so sexy and looked so vulnerable. He saw the limo driver checking them both out in his rearview mirror. The thought of him watching them turned Nick on even more. He turned to Isabelle and kissed her gently. Her body responded straight away to his touch. He slid his hand under her top and started caressing her breast gently, till she started moaning and arched her body. God she looked so sexy. He pulled her top down and kissed her nipples. They instantly got hard and he knew she was horny and wanted him… the driver kept on watching them in his mirror.

"Do you like her?" Nick asked him.

"Yes. Ah…no sir. I'm sorry sir."

"So you don't want to touch her?"

"No sir." The driver looked away embarrassed.

Isabelle opened her eyes in shock. What the hell was happening. Wow! She felt something was wrong. She looked at Nick and pulled her top back up.

"Are you insane?" she asked.

"You are mine babe. I am yours, and this is all that matters." He kept on playing with her.

"Nick, stop…"

He pulled her top down again and squished her nipple a bit stronger this time. The driver, still watching.

"You are beautiful baby. Does it feel good?" He squished her nipple even harder and bit her softly on her neck. "You know… Ms. Lucardi…you look sexy as hell. Is this ok, or you want me to stop?" He leaned forwards and kissed her, while he gently pushed her legs open.

"Nick…no…stop…"

He pushed aside her knickers and slid his fingers into her pussy. It was soaking wet. He spread her pussy open some more and found his way to her clitoris. Isabelle was gone. He had total control over her now and he knew it. He enjoyed it. He looked at the mirror and saw the driver's eyes. Fuck he felt high and horny. He was so turned on, he could barely stop himself from coming…but he was going to make her come. She was his. Isabelle Lucardi belonged to him…Nicholas Walters. She was asking for it and begging him to give it to her. Desperate for the sweet release and joy of the climax.

"Tell me you are mine, Isabelle. Are you mine?"

"Yes Nick."

"Show me you are mine. Give yourself to me. Give me everything you have. Now!"

"Nick, no. Please…"

"Let yourself go. Come for me baby."

He pushed two fingers inside her and she cried out loud.

"Quiet honey." Nick chided.

He found her clitoris and started playing with it.

She called his name loudly and exploded in his hand. She couldn't resist the desire and tension any more. She came right there, on the back seat of the limo, with the limo driver watching her in the mirror.

The car stopped in front of the building and they got out.

Nick made love to her passionately that night back in the apartment. She gave him everything and responded to every touch and every kiss.

It was magical…it was love!

The next day Nick went to the office, just for an hour. It was a Saturday.

"These are for you" he said, coming back in holding a beautiful bouquet of roses.

"They are beautiful!"

"So are you, my darling!" he kissed her gently. "I can't believe you're still in bed! It's 11am!"

"I was waiting for you!" she smiled seductively.

"You don't have to ask me twice!"

He started to get undressed but she jumped out of the bed and ran past him, locking herself in the bathroom.

"I was only joking!" she giggled from the inside.

"Please let me in darling! Please!" He could hear the shower running.

"I need to take a shower too!"

"After me babe! Ladies first!"

"What about taking a shower together?"

"That will take far too long, and I am starving. You need to feed me Mr. Walters" she said laughing.

They made spaghetti at home and Isabelle showed him how to cook the best tomato sauce.

"But please, don't start imagining I'm going to be doing this for you every day from now on!" she said watching him licking the sauce spoon.

"How about if I pay you to do it…with love and kisses!"

"That's an offer I might just consider!"

"So, what do you want to do today darling?" he asked. "We can go for a ride or stay at home and watch movies. We are going out to 'Tao' tonight."

"Are we meeting someone there?"

"Yes, Gilberto and Nicola, from last night."

They spent the afternoon then, watching movies, being lazy and making love.

"I've never been to Tao before, but I have heard it's similar to 'Buddha Bar' in Paris." she said.

"Yes, it is, only bigger, like everything in New York. You'll like it and if not…we go somewhere else."

"You are the best man in the world" she squeezed his hand "…and I love you."

Gilberto and Nicola turned up a little bit later.

"Here you are, you love birds!" Gil liked to joke with Nick.

"Where did you disappear to last night? I turned around and you were both gone."

"Isabelle was tired…and I needed to give her a…foot massage!" Everybody laughed…a foot massage!!!

"I'll take one of those again tonight please" Isabelle added.

"It will be my pleasure, honey…anything for you!"

The restaurant was impressive. There were two levels with an open courtyard in the middle. The second floor had open balconies looking down to the courtyard. On the first floor, there was a bar, right next to the main entrance. At the far end you could see the stone statue of Buddha, which was so big, his head reached up to the ceiling of the building.

"It's breathtaking!" Isabelle whispered to Nick "and all these candles…it looks like a temple!"

"Ladies, what are you having to drink? Bottle of wine or are we doing cocktails?" Gil asked.

"Bottle of wine!" they replied in unison.

The night went quickly. The food was good, the wine was excellent, the music was great, and Nick was there.

"Shall we make a call to Bob?" Gil asked Nick.

"Who's Bob?" Isabelle asked.

"A drug dealer" Nicola answered her question.

Isabelle looked in shock at Nick…but once the thought had been planted in her mind… it was too late to turn back.

"Well, let's call him!" she said.

Bob showed up twenty minutes later. He'd brought a couple of packs of cocaine and a few ecstasy pills.

"You look like a pharmacist!" Gilberto joked with him.

They left the restaurant and went to 'Pm.' for a drink. Nick and Isabelle disappeared to the bathroom.

"Where did they go?" Nicola asked.

"Taking care of business!" Gil explained to her. "They went for a line Silly! Do you want some?"

He gave her a hug. Gil and Nicola had been together for years and he always liked to drive her mad.

Nick came back and got a bottle of Grey Goose for the table. The night was turning into a heavy one!

"I would like some Cranberry juice and some Red bull please" he gave his order to the cute waitress who couldn't stop staring at him.

The stuff Bob had brought turned to be quite good and everybody was flying. Isabelle was dancing and Nick started to feel exactly the way he'd felt when she'd given him his first dance in 'Scores'.

"Stop! Stop! I won´t let you torture me like that ever again!" He laughed and pushed her down onto the leather couch. "…not in public, when I can't do anything about it!"

"I've never seen him acting like this with a woman." Nicola sat next to Isabelle. "What have you done to him?"

"Nothing! The question is, what has he done to me? I'm like hypnotized, but I love it! I love every second of being with him. I want him for always, you'll see, one day…I will marry him!"

"He'll be a good catch" Nicola smiled "his ex wasn't the right one for him and he wasn't happy around her, but look at him now…he's dancing for God's sake!"

They both laughed, watching him moving clumsily to the music. One thing was sure…Nick was not a dancer.

"Why did they break up, him and his ex?" Isabelle asked.

If Nicola was willing to speak, she wouldn't say no to finding something about Nick, because he never talked about himself. "She was older than him and she was at the point where she wanted to get married and have some kids…Nick wasn't ready. They were together for two years."

That was good to know, Isabelle thought. She would've never asked Nick about his ex, but she was curious about it.

"Come on girls! Stop talking. Don't join forces against us.

We love you!" Gil interrupted them "Ready for another drink?"

"I am!" Isabelle said, "and for a shot too!"

Nick mixed her a vodka cranberry and sat next to her.

"You make me so happy babe. I´ve been waiting for you all my life…everyone said 'real love doesn't exist' but I believed and never settled for less! And now you are here! I found you, my love!" His voice was quiet.

"I wanted exactly the same." Isabelle replied.

"I didn't want to settle down with someone for whatever reason. I knew that if I was patient, I'd meet the right man for me, who would give me everything I needed and would make me the happiest woman in the world. Someone, who would love me for who I am. Someone like you babe!"

She looked in his eyes and could see the love pouring out of them. They were back again in their own perfect world. Just the two of them. "Shall we go back to yours?" Gil interrupted "we can take the bottle with us and get the hell out of here… Let's go!"

It was hard to do drugs in a night club. You need to go to the bathroom all the time and there was always a queue.

By the time Gilberto and Nicola left to go home it was 6 am. And by the time Nick and Isabelle went to sleep it was 7 am.

They spent the whole Sunday in bed.

"I'm not drinking vodka ever again" Isabelle said.

"You said that last time, remember?"

"This time I mean it!"

"I'm sure, you do, till next Friday!"

He tickled her to cheer her up, but her hangover was killing her.

"Damn, my head feels like a washing machine! Do you feel the same, or is it just me?"

"I feel bad too, but I knew I'd feel like it before I even started yesterday, so I am not complaining."

"I am not good with pain and suffering." she said. "Do you have something for a headache? I need an Alka-Seltzer and half a Valium, so I can lay back and chill."

"You are not getting any of it. You'll kill yourself with all these pills. We partied last night and you felt great, today it hurts a little, but this is the price to pay. All you are getting from me is a cheeseburger, cause you need to eat and lots of water' he gave her a kiss.

"Yes daddy" she moaned and went to take a shower.

He reached for the phone and was about to dial the number for the food delivery, when he heard the screams. He ran into the bathroom and found her in the shower her eyes wide open, filled with panic.

"What happened?" He jumped into the shower still in his clothes.

"What the fuck happened?" he repeated.

"Did we make love last night?" she asked.

"What?"

"Did we have sex?" She repeated herself.

"Yes, we did!"

"I just remembered…" she almost started sobbing. "I must've been so drunk…where did you come Nick?" Her eyes were fixed on his now.

"Did you come inside me?" her voice was threatening.

"You made me do it." He defended himself, "you begged me to do it…and I did it."

She pushed him away.

"Are you seriously telling me you did that? You know I'm not taking anything to protect myself and neither are you! So, what the fuck were you thinking? What if I get pregnant? I wouldn't have an abortion, and I am not ready for a baby either. That's not something you should be joking about, Nick."

He could see it in her eyes, that she was serious.

"Let's hope nothing has happened this time." She calmed down a bit. "But please don't play with fire, because you might get burned!"

She came out of the shower and left him there by himself…under the hot water, still wearing his shorts and t-shirt. She was really angry with him.

Isabelle had told him, she'd had two abortions and the doctors had warned her, a third would not be a good idea if she ever wanted to have kids…and she wanted kids. A boy and a girl! She loved Nick, but they'd only known each other for a brief time. To make a step like that, she had to be hundred percent sure…and she wasn't there yet.

"Listen, I'm really sorry." Nick came out of the bathroom. "I won't do it again, I promise."

He was looking so sad and worried, it broke her heart seeing him this way. So, she waved away all her bad thoughts and put her arms around him.

"I forgive you, just be more careful."

"I'll call my doctor friend tomorrow and ask him to write you a prescription for the morning after pill." He was back smiling again.

He ordered some food, which they ate in bed, watching

a movie. Then later that afternoon, they went out for a walk, to get some fresh air.

She wasn't going back to her apartment till Monday. Frank had flown back to Florida and wasn't coming back till the following week.

"Do you ice skate?" Nick asked, "If you want, next weekend instead of going out getting wasted on Saturday, we should stay in and get up early on Sunday and I'll take you for breakfast and after that ice skating in Central Park!" The look on her face was priceless.

"Really? Is that a promise?"

"It's a promise!"

Chapter 19

The week flew by, like in a second.

Isabelle started to spend more and more time with Nick. She even stayed at his place on some of the weekdays after work and cuddle up next to him in his bed. Then he'd come back home from the office at 12 o'clock, bringing her a latte from Starbucks and to wake her up with kisses. Everything was almost too good to be true.

On Friday night, they went out for dinner to Le Colonial, the French Vietnamese restaurant and went to bed early.

She woke up with a smile on Saturday. Nick had told her that he had surprise for her for that evening. She took a quick shower and left the house. It was a beautiful day, and a beautiful day to pamper herself with her beauty routine…a manicure, a pedicure, a facial and a blow-dry. When she came back home around 2.30 pm and Nick was already there, waiting for her.

"You look beautiful!" he said.

They drove down to Battery Park and walked around the water, Nick guiding her round the points of interest, the Statue of Liberty the most notable of course.

They had lunch in a small Italian restaurant and if they were not eating, talking or walking, they were kissing each other. The love was in the air, for all to witness.

"Tomorrow we're going ice skating remember" he said on the way back home. "Tonight, if you want, we should stay local and check out the bars in the area. There is a Latino club across the street, an Irish pub next to it or we could go to the 'Wet Bar' down the block."

So the early night turned into another early morning, again. Bob had come to see them a few times that night and Gilberto had been there at one point too and must have left in the early hours. There was an empty vodka bottle on the kitchen counter and packs of cigarettes lying around everywhere.

She opened her eyes and checked the time…6 pm. on Sunday!

"Fuck! What have we done?"

She looked at Nick, who was fast asleep next to her.

"Nick, wake up, wake up…it's six in the afternoon, we've slept the whole day."

Her head was killing her. She walked out to the living room, only to find the mess they'd created throughout the night. The air was stinky, filled with smoke and alcohol. Isabelle opened the balcony door to let in the fresh, cold November air.

Nick woke up in a bad mood too, but at least he wasn't showing it so obviously. He tried to start a conversation with her, but she was blocking all his attempts, concentrating on cleaning up the house.

"I'd better give her a half a valium today" he thought to himself "before she blames it all on me for feeling like this and decides to murder me!"

Isabelle carried on tidying up the house, she put all the glasses in the dish washer, emptied the ashtrays and changed the bed sheets, as there was cigarette ash all over them too.

"What did we do? Why didn't you stop it?" she cried out "we were supposed to go ice skating…"

"Oh, oh" he sighed to himself "where's the valium? I better give her a whole one."

He took a little blue pill and tried to give it to her.

"Take this, it'll make you feel better. It'll ease your hangover." "Get away from me with all your drugs." She screamed at him.

He didn't give up though, he was familiar with the situation. In his experience he found women always got bitchy the day after they'd partied. It was even worse than when they were having their period.

"It's an aspirin honey, extra strong" He brought a glass of water.

"Drink it and you'll feel better!"

She grabbed the pill and without even looking at it, swallowed it.

"Thank God!" Nick whispered under his breath.

It would take half an hour to take effect and then she'd calm down. All he could do for now was to stay quiet and wait.

He turned the TV on and glanced at his watch, 7.30 pm…she'd be ok by 8. He took a half a pill and smiled whilst thinking to himself , "Women…why do they take drugs and drink when they don't know how to handle it…?"

Half an hour later, as he'd predicted, she joined him on the sofa and snuggled against his body. He let her lay in his arms without saying anything and stroked her hair. She was asleep in twenty minutes. He carried her to bed and kissed her gently good night. He stayed there in the darkness of the room for a moment and watched her sleeping, she looked like an angel.

Chapter 20

Time was passing quickly, Christmas was approaching. Nick invited her to the office Christmas party and Isabelle invited him to spend Christmas with her and her dad in Mallorca.

The company Christmas party was taking place in Long Island. They'd hired a limo for the night. Nick wore a black Canali suit and she'd dressed in black Versace trousers and a sleeveless white top from Chanel. They both looked very classy and extremely elegant.

Nick introduced her to all his work colleagues. She enjoyed the way he displayed his affection for her in front of everybody. He always made sure she was by his side and when he was talking to someone, he always included her in the conversation. She got to meet the other girlfriends and wives of Nick's friends too and they all seemed to like her.

They were sitting next to the bar when Nick said, "This is where I was used to bartend, right here in Long Island… oh, those were crazy times! I was going to school to get my broker license during the day and worked behind the bar, during the night…"

"And when did you sleep?" Isabelle asked.

"I didn't! That's when I started doing drugs. It was a substitute for espresso. We used to call it 'American coffee'" he laughed,

"I bartended for about seven years before I started to make money through trading, and with the way it's continuing to go now, I should be very rich pretty soon."

Nick's company was opening a new office downtown and Nick and his partner were going to be co-owners with fifty percent each one. This was a big opportunity for them both and they knew it. Both of them young and successful, exactly what everybody dreamt about. He looked at her and kissed her forehead.

"And if we're still together, you'll never have to work another day in your life again."

He hated her job, and she knew it. They never talked about it, but she knew it. She needed the money and he couldn't offer it to her at that moment, so silently, they had agreed not to talk about it. She wanted to go into the fashion business. She and her sister had had that dream since they were little girls.

"What are you dreaming about?" Nick asked.

"I'm dreaming about a dream!" she said and leaned her head against his shoulder.

They went back home and made love again and again, until they fell asleep in each other arms.

Chapter 21

Things in 'Scores' were getting a little out of control. It was Christmas time and there were girls coming from all over America to work in the club, around a hundred and fifty girls every night. It was just too much.

Jordan wasn't happy about it. The dressing room was overcrowded. There was never even one empty space at the bar. The women were everywhere. She and Gaby were making money, but they were getting tired of all the hassle. It sure was time for a vacation.

She was leaving for Spain in a week, and she wanted to take as much cash as she could.

"Hey Jordan" Gaby said, "do you want to go talk to the guys over there with me?"

"Sure, why not."

They had both been drinking the whole night. Jordan had lost count of how many martinis she'd had.

"Do you have any charlie?" she asked Gaby.

"Girl, watch yourself! Someone might hear you…"

"Ok, ok…but do you have any?"

"No, but I have someone coming in an hour and bringing me some proper good stuff. If you want, we can share a bag!"

"Cool, how much do you want for it?"

"Fifty bucks!"

The two guys had just finished their dinner. They ordered drinks for the girls and half an hour later they'd all moved to the champagne lounge. By 2 am Jordan could barely stand on her feet. The drugs were gone, and she was feeling sick. They'd made lots of money from the guys, but she was feeling so bad she told Gaby she had to go.

"There is nothing for free in this fucking world!" said Gaby. It was hard to understand Gaby, as she was very drunk too.

They were getting changed in the dressing room. There was no point for either of them to stay any longer. They'd made over a thousand dollars each and if they had even just one more drink, one of them would've fallen over and the other would've probably thrown up in the middle of the showroom. The manager let them go straight away after seeing the condition they were in.

"This is the part I hate most about this job" Isabelle stated, "I love the money...don't even mind getting topless in front of all these men, but what kills me is the alcohol!"

"Stop drinking then!" said Gaby.

"Yeah right!!!" said Jordan, "Work in a strip club and not drink. How can you talk to all these people, when they're all drunk...and who wants to talk to a prudish sober stripper?"

"No one!" replied Gaby.

"You said it!" agreed Jordan.

"What are you doing now? Are you going home or going to see Nick?" Gaby asked and gave her a smile. "I can't believe

you guys are still together. It's great! I'm so happy for you."
"Thanks! I'm happy for myself too." They both laughed.

"No, I think I will go home. I'm too drunk and I might get sick and that wouldn't be very romantic, would it?!" said Jordan.

She gave Gaby a hug and went home.

She did get sick the minute she got into the apartment. Thank God, she hadn't gone to Nick's, she thought…it would've been so embarrassing. Frank was in Florida, so there was no one else to witness her condition. She didn't even call Nick to let him know she was at home safe.

"I'll deal with all that tomorrow" she said to herself and passed out on her bed, still fully clothed.

There were ten missed calls on her cell phone the next morning. All from Nick. She dialed his number.

"You're alive!!! I was so worried about you…where have you been?" he yelled at her.

For the first time she felt some kind of aggression in his voice.

"Calm down" she said, "I'm fine, at home, just waking up. I was too tired last night to come to yours and I forgot to call you. I'm sorry…I really am sorry honey."

"You should be!" his voice was still filled with anger "What time did you get back home ? If you went home at all?"

"What are you talking about? Are you completely crazy? I had a few drinks last night and left the club around three o'clock. So don't be stupid! I wouldn't go anywhere to party without you babe. I love you and only you."

She could hear him breathing heavily on the other end of the phone. She'd really had no idea that Nick was that jealous. He'd never shown any signs of it before.

She pulled her blanket to herself and dark clouds entered her mind.

Jealousy was a disease, a terribly bad and dangerous one.

Chapter 22

The car was going at high speed. They were late. The Delta flight to Barcelona was leaving in less than two hours. She'd known they were going to be late…

She'd been getting ready to leave for the airport and Nick was coming to pick her up. He should've waited downstairs in the car instead of coming up. Once he was in the apartment, it had been too late to save the situation.

She'd been fixing her hair in the bathroom, when he came behind her and pressed his hot lips to her neck. Desire had exploded through her body.

He pushed her legs open.

"We are going to be late, I can't miss my flight," she whispered with a husky voice.

"Shht, don't speak."

"But…"

"Shht." His hand covered her mouth.

"Open your legs for me…wider."

She did what he said. He put his fingers between her legs and slid them into her pussy. She was soaking wet.

"I love this pussy wet like that. Is this how much you want me?" He started playing with her, his fingers searching out and finding her clitoris, she arched her body, opening herself even wider to him.

"Oh God, don't stop." She cried out with desire.

"Do you like it…does it feel good, my darling?"

He put his other hand on her nipples and started touching them, first one and then the other, pulling them gently.

Isabelle looked at her reflection in the mirror and barely recognized the woman she saw there. She was transfixed.

"You are my bitch, remember that. You are mine. I love seeing you like that, totally losing yourself in the pleasure. Tell me you want me."

"Oh yes baby, I do. I do with every inch of my body."

"Will you do as I tell you to?"

"Anything you want Nick, just don't stop, please. I will give you everything you want. I will give you all of myself. I am yours, only yours and only you can make me feel this way. "

"Touch yourself and watch in the mirror while you're doing it."

He was playing with both her nipples now and she was totally lost in the ecstasy of it.

"Don't come yet. You will come when I tell you to. Do you understand.?"

"Yes."

"I want you to suck my cock. Turn around."

"Oh no, don't stop…" she pleaded.

"Now please. Nice and gently. Show it some love. All the way down." He was caressing her hair. "That's my girl…Do you want that cock inside you?"

"Yes please."

"Then make it really hard for yourself."

She moaned with pleasure. Nick then lifted her up onto her feet and swung her around again. He opened her butt cheeks, licked his finger and put it gently inside. Isabelle let out a little cry.

"It will hurt a bit, but the pain can be nice too. Just don't scream." He put his hand over her mouth again. "I love you. You need to trust me. I will never hurt you. You are my baby. Tell me you are mine."

"I am yours. Take me please." She begged him.

He put his hand on her pussy and pushed his fingers in, playing with her clitoris. With his other hand he pushed his cock gently into her behind. She screamed. From pleasure and pain at the same time.

"You can come now. Come for me baby. Let me see your face. Just like that. You look so beautiful. Christ Isabelle! I want you. I want you so much! I can't live without you."

He'd taken her right there, in the bathroom…and now they were late.

They were getting closer to the airport, but Isabelle was getting increasingly anxious.

"I can't lose this flight. My ticket is a fixed one. Not changeable, non refundable. If I lose this flight, you will be buying me a new ticket."

"Do I get to do what I did again then?" he smiled at her.

"Stop it, it's not funny, I have a connection to make in Barcelona and there are not that many flights going to Mallorca in the wintertime."

It was funny for him but he was driving as fast as he could.

Nick was going to join Isabelle at the end of the week. They were going to spend their first Christmas together in Mallorca. The ticket was booked, and she'd even helped him pack his suitcase.

"So, I'll see you on Saturday!" she said.

"Make sure you don't forget to pick me up from the airport, because I will find you Ms. Lucardi and make you pay for that…"

"If you don't shut up, I might really do that… I kind of like the idea!"

They arrived at John F. Kennedy airport just in time for her to catch her flight.

She looked at him, after passing through security and blew him a kiss.

"I love you!" she shouted.

"I love you even more honey… to the moon and back!" he replied.

Chapter 23

Spain welcomed her with sunshine and relatively good weather. Carlos picked her up from the airport.

"How's my girl?"

"She's fine and how's her dad?"

"Getting older."

"Oh, please, don't make me laugh." She gave him a kiss on the cheek.

"So, when is your boyfriend coming?" Carlos asked her.

"Saturday. I'm picking him up from the airport 'round lunch time."

Her phone rang. It was Frank.

"Are you in Spain already? I tried the apartment and your cell phone, but there was no answer, so I figured I'd find you on your Spanish number."

"I just landed. Dad's here right next to me and we're on the way home."

"Say hi to Carlos for me. I only called to wish you a Merry Christmas. I'm taking my family on one of those Disney Cruise ships for ten days and my phone will be off.

So Merry Christmas and a Happy New Year to you and Carlos and we'll speak again next year."

"Carlos says hello back. All the best to you and your family and I'll see you next year."

The house was just the way she'd left it. She hurried in and called her best friend Peter.

"I'm back!"

"Oh God help me! The Devil is back in town!" Peter and Isabelle had been friends for quite a long time.

They used to be inseparable and really cared about each other.

He owned a nice little restaurant in Palma, and she had thought about going there with Carlos tonight but she had lots of things to do in the next couple of days, so maybe not tonight.

Her thoughts went back to New York. She smiled, thinking about Nick and what he did to her in the bathroom.

The next morning she woke up early and drove to Palma. She hadn't had any energy to leave her sofa the night before.

Peter was in his restaurant, preparing for the day.

"One day, you'll die in here!" she said, "Working too much has never been a healthy thing."

"Lucardi, mind your own business!"

He grabbed her in his arms and gave her a big fat kiss.

"I've been missing you, young lady…since you got all loved up in the Big City, I barely hear from you anymore. Your dad told me you were back here in November, but I guess you forgot to call me."

"That's right, but I can explain…"

He stretched his arm and placed his hand a millimeter from her nose.

"Habla con la mano!" he said "talk to the hand! Anyway, what's the plan now?"

"I invited Nick over for Christmas, Carlos, me, and you. Will you cook dinner for us, I will be your apprentice!"

"Lucardi, you never listen to me when I talk to you, do you? I told you already on the phone, the restaurant is open on Christmas Eve and on Christmas day. I cannot come to your party, and I can't cook for you either. You'll have to come up with another plan. Or you can come here if you want, then I will cook for you. That's all I can do for now."

"I'll think about it." said Isabelle

"Thinking is for the donkeys, because they have big heads." and he made a funny face.

They both laughed. Peter was always there for her when she needed him. She could call him at any time and he would listen to her, always on her side. She really appreciated his friendship.

Isabelle spent the rest of the day talking on the phone and shopping. She'd called her mom and her sister, talked to Nick a few times and all the rest of her friends in Mallorca. She'd also spent hours in El Corte Ingles on Jaime III, downtown Palma, picking up Christmas decorations.

"It's going to be my first Christmas at home and the first one with Nick" she said to herself and she wanted so much, that things worked out perfectly. She was so happy and prayed every day that this happiness continued.

Carlos took her for an early dinner, down at the port.

"What shall we do for Christmas Eve dinner?" she asked him.

"I don't know, why don't you cook something?"

"Dad, you are talking to me here… about cooking!"

"Call your mother and ask her for some good tips and recipes."

He was going too far now. He knew damn well her mother didn't cook either.

"I'm serious dad. I can't serve salad with spaghetti on Christmas Eve and that's all I'm capable of."

"I'll speak to Antonio when he brings the bill. We'll figure something out baby girl! Leave it to daddy!"

"Well then, I must go. I'm meeting Peter for a little catch up."

"Be a good girl and don't drink too much. I'll check up on you later."

She kissed him on his cheek and ran to meet Peter.

"When will she finally grow up?" he thought to himself.

He would love to see her settled down and married, but most of all he would like to have a grandchild. He liked what he heard about Nick and was looking forward to meeting him. He was the first of her boyfriends who seemed reasonable and down to earth and they were both around the same age. He couldn't wait to meet him personally. Who knows, he could possibly be the one for his little girl. Antonio came with bill and dragged him out of his thoughts.

"Toni, can you cook something for us for Christmas Eve? Isabelle has invited her boyfriend and wants to surprise him."

"For you, of course. What would you like?"

"I'll leave it up to you…just make it nice."

So, Christmas dinner was organized. He smiled and finished his wine. Carlos liked his drink. Sometimes he worried about Isabelle, drinking too much. She was her father's daughter and the apple doesn't fall too far from the tree.

"I need to talk to her about all this…she is my little girl, and she needs to be more careful." He thought to himself.

If he only knew about the dancing, the alcohol and the drugs. If he only knew, he would've had a heart attack, right there and then. But don't all parents want the best of their children? Isabelle was his only child and he wanted her to be happy, that was all. Her mom got remarried after they got divorced, but he never did. He didn't want Isabelle to end up being alone like him. He knew what it was to be lonely.

At the other end of the port, Isabelle was having a drink with Peter. They were having a laugh. She was telling him about Nick and the way they met.

"Typical Lucardi!" he said, "You can't meet a man in the supermarket, for example, but you have to meet one when you are drunk and can't see further than your nose. Man, oh man." She couldn't stop laughing.

"Did you recognize him the next time you saw him? Because we both know sometimes, you don't remember a thing the day after?"

"No, not at first glance. I had to look twice to make sure it was him."

He laughed too.

"Did you figure out yet what you are doing for Christmas Eve? I'm running out of tables at the restaurant."

"I want to stay home. I promised myself this when I first bought the place and I've been looking forward to it since then.

It's going to be my first Christmas in my own house, in my dream house actually."

"I understand! I'll come by tomorrow morning before work and help you decorate the tree."

"There's no tree yet!"

"Well, we go and buy a tree first and then I'll help you decorate it."

"That's a deal Peter Pan." Isabelle said, delighted with the plan.

"I'll come to pick you up at eleven. Please be ready."

Peter did as he promised. They had to check a few stores, till they found what they were looking for…a six foot tall tree, unfortunately, a plastic one. They put it together and Peter helped her to decorate it. They put Christmas lights and candles everywhere. The house looked beautiful.

"I think, we deserve a drink," she said and disappeared in the kitchen.

"Not for me, I'm off to work."

"OK, I'll see you later then…and Pete" she paused "can you organize some of those MDMA pills for me?"

MDMA was more or less the same as ecstasy. She knew Nick would love them.

"I see, what I can do." said Peter.

Chapter 24

Isabelle was staring at the flight information screen. Nick's flight was supposed to land any minute. She was so excited. It had been a week already since she'd seen him. They'd spoken on the phone a lot, but it wasn't the same. She couldn't wait to hold him and kiss him.

His flight info on the screen began to blink and showed that the flight from Madrid had just landed. Nick was finally here.

She hurried to gate B. It took him ages to collect his luggage, but eventually he turned up. She felt so nervous about seeing him, but he just grabbed her, kissed her passionately and instantly she felt a million times better being there in his arms.

"I've missed you so much and I am really happy you are here." she managed to say.

They were driving down the Paseo Maritimo. Isabelle didn't take the bypass on purpose. She drove through Palma, so he could have a look at the city and get a right feeling for the island.

"It's beautiful babe. I envy you for living here." Nick said.

"I don't live here full time remember, I spend the half of the year in New York with you!" she laughed.

"Now I envy you, even more, because you have picked the best of the world and have made it your home."

They got to her house and his mouth dropped open in amazement.

"Wow, now I understand when you say, you miss home. This place rocks baby!"

He went out on the terrace admiring the views.

"There's a terrace on the roof too." she said, "Come on, I'll show you."

She took his hand, and they went up the spiral staircase. It was huge and the view from there was even more breath taking. In front was the Mediterranean Sea, as far as you could see, to the left, he could see all the way to Palma and to the right side were the sandy beaches of Palma Nova.

"And these are the Calvia mountains" she pointed to the back.

"This is amazing, I'm really impressed," he kissed her gently "and proud of you." he added.

They spend the day organizing the last details for their dinner. Antonio had baked some ham for them, with potatoes and green beans for the main course and for a starter, Isabelle had made one of her special salads, topped with a lemon dressing. They had stocked up on both red and white wine too. Nick helped her to set the table, it felt like they were a real family. She had put his present under the tree and he had done the same with hers. There were boxes there from Peter and her dad as well. She was so happy, she was dancing around the house.

Carlos arrived at eight o'clock and had brought the dessert with him. A cake, he'd ordered especially two days before in Café Pastel, a French patisserie in Portals Nous.

She looked at the two men and her heart sank.

"I have everything I want right here in front of me," she thought, "I just wish that my mom and my sister were here too!"

But she knew they had their own families and these two men were hers. Her eyes filled with tears and trying to hide them, she ran into the kitchen, pretending to be looking for something.

"Do you need some help honey?" Nick asked.

"No, I'm ok. Just looking for serviettes."

"They're already on the table."

They said a prayer of thanks and tasted their food. Toni had done an excellent job.

"Do you want to go out after dinner?" she asked Nick "We can all go to Wellies in the Port. I want you to meet one my of best friends, Peter."

"That sounds great." Nick replied.

Carlos really liked Nick, and it looked like the young man was in love with his daughter. Nick came across as a very gentle and kind man. There was not a bad word to come out of his mouth. He was very patient and laid back with not a trace of any sign of aggression. Nick seemed to be a real good guy.

They all went to Wellies an hour later. Peter was still not there. Nick bought everybody a drink. He was talking to Carlos at the bar, trying to put himself in an even better light. They were discussing the latest movements of the stock market, a boring subject for Isabelle.

"Are you here for a while?" Carey, the girl behind the bar, asked Isabelle.

"I'll be here for new Year's Eve. Nick is flying back to New York on Tuesday. He has meetings on Wednesday and Thursday." "Oh, God! That is so silly. He should cancel them. Flying all the way here and at the end leaving you alone on New Year's Eve. That's stupid."

Isabelle stared at her for a long, long moment. She had never thought about it in this way. She trusted Nick about everything. Never questioned his decisions. Never doubted what he was telling her…Maybe she was too naïve…What if he was playing her? The thought started to make her feel uncomfortable.

He had all the opportunities. They were not living together. She was working during the week, so he knew there was no chance of her showing up at his door unexpectedly. He was in his office all day, every day and anytime he wouldn't answer his phone for hours, he would just say he was in a meeting.

Anyway, why did he really need so desperately to fly back to New York over New Year, to work for two days? This really did not make a lot of sense. She felt her stomach turning itself upside down.

"What if he is playing the fucking game of love with me?" She didn't realize she had said this out loud.

"Test him! " Carey said.

"No! I don't want to test anything or anybody. I'll let it go for now and just keep my eyes open. Time will tell!"

Peter turned up around midnight and brought five MDMA pills. Carlos left shortly after and left the three of them at the bar. Nick liked Peter, but Peter wasn't extremely impressed with Nick.

"Have you noticed how possessive of you, he is?" he asked Isabelle.

"He just loves me." She tried to defend Nick.

"That isn't love, Lucardi. He acts as if he owns you. Look, how nervous he gets when someone only says "Hello" to you."

"He's only just arrived Pete! Give him some time to get used in here. It's unfamiliar territory for him and he's being protective of me."

They never said another word about it again.

The three of them shared the pills and hit the clubs in Palma. First, they went to Pascha on the Paseo Maritimo and afterwards Peter took them to a place called SixtyThree, a proper after hours club, somewhere on the Plaza Gomilla, the redlight district of Palma.

The pills had worked their magic on Isabelle. Her mind wasn't working anymore and she had no idea what was she doing.

"I think you'd better take her home now" Peter suggested to Nick.

Isabelle was dancing next to them. It was dark inside and the smoke was thick. Everyone was high on either cocaine or ecstasy. It was a typical underground joint.

Peter looked at her. Tomorrow, she wouldn't even remember she'd been there. Now she had to go home. He took her hand and led her out of the club. Nick followed them. Peter put them both in a taxi and gave the driver Isabelle's address.

"There is something wrong with this guy" he thought to himself about Nick, but he just couldn't figure out what!

He didn't want to see Isabelle hurt and it seemed to him, that Nick was going to do exactly that.

Nick and Isabelle stayed in all Christmas Day. They used the time to catch up on kissing each other and making love all day long. They opened their presents, watched movies and lay around naked. Isabelle had long forgotten about all the warning signs that had been blinking red in her head the night before. She was letting herself sink deeper and deeper into the sea of love. She was opening her heart more and more for Nick with every minute. He was the best man in the world, period.

"I love you." She kissed him gently on the lips.

"With you, I feel myself. I feel understood and loved. I feel so complete since you came into my life…I honestly do." she said.

"I love you too honey. I'm sorry I wasn't here to help you decorate the house and put the tree together, but I promise you I'll be here next Christmas. From now on, wherever we go, we should pick up an ornament from every place for our Christmas tree as a souvenir to remember. Imagine our tree in twenty years."

She closed her eyes and saw it. She saw them both, twenty years older, sitting next to a big Christmas tree, holding each other the same way, they were holding each other right in this moment. They were in each other's future, she thought, sure that Nick saw the same thing.

They talked about, what they are going to do with their lives. She was surprised how similar their dreams were.

They shared the same moral code and had the same values. Sometimes she had the feeling that someone had told Nick all about her, and now he had all the right answers to all the questions you could possibly ask.

"I need to stop looking for faults in him," she thought "It's almost like I don't want him to be as good as he actually is. God, please don't let me fuck this up. I've never been this happy in my life and I want it to stay this way."

He was holding her in his arms. They felt asleep like this, on the floor in front of the fireplace. Nick woke up a few hours later and carried her to bed.

Chapter 25

Monday came and went so quickly, they barely noticed it.

"Why don't you stay one more day?" she said, "You can leave on Wednesday and go to the office on Thursday and Friday."

"No, I can't. We just opened the new office, and I cannot leave my partner alone. They need me there." "I need you too" she whispered in his ear.

They went out to Palma in the afternoon and walked down the small streets in La Llonja. Isabelle took him to a place called Abaco, an old house, transformed into a bar. It was a very extraordinary experience. There were thousands of real fruits spread all around the floors and the bars, flowers everywhere, bird cages in the winter garden. They ordered champagne and she showed him around the house. It was like a museum. There were paintings from famous artists on the walls, all the furniture represented the era of French Baroque.

"What do you think about it?" she asked.

"It's brilliant, never seen anything like this before." Nick replied.

They finished their drinks and hit the streets again. Later, she brought Nick to Peter's restaurant for dinner. They tried some of the dishes from his expansive menu and picked up another five MDMA.

"If he doesn't want to stay another day, then he better stay up the whole night with me and make it up for the day" she said to herself.

She didn't need to twist his arm to take it. They swallowed the first two already in the restaurant.

"These pills are really good," she said to Pete. "Where do you get them from?"

"My friend sends them to me in the post every now and again, directly from Amsterdam. That's why they're so good. What you get in the States is the MDMA powder mixed up with something else but my shit is pure."

"Ask your friend if he can send me some of these to New York!" Nick laughed.

The alcohol was flowing again, and the pills were starting to kick in. Isabelle was getting high and tipsy, but she had no desire to end up in an after hours hole, like the last time.

"Shall we make a move?" she asked Nick, "I rather go back home and open a bottle of wine there, chill and relax."

"Sure!" Nick thought of her naked and asked for the check straight away.

He'd started to take her clothes off already in the lift, so by the time they locked the door to the apartment behind them, he had no pants on and she had no shirt. They had wild and frantic sex and that's where things went out of control, again. He couldn't stop himself and he didn't want to pull himself out of her, so he let himself explode inside her.

"What are you doing?" she cried out.

It was too late... he had come already.

"I love you" he whispered and pulled her back to his chest. "If God wants you to get pregnant, it will happen anyway."

"Honey, this is not a roulette game here! And what does God have to do with all this? I'm not on the pill, you don't use a condom and you keep on coming inside me. One plus one makes two, don't you think? The chance of me getting pregnant increases every time we make love, and you forget to take it out."

She had to laugh at her own speech. Why was she angry at all? She loved the man, the man loved her, and he was old enough to know what he was doing.

"It's not like I didn't tell you. I did warn you...if I get pregnant, we are going to have a baby and nothing in the whole wide world would make me change my mind."

"Yes, I know this." He stopped her from talking with a kiss.

They did not sleep a wink the whole night. Took the rest of the pills and finished all the bottles of wine she had stocked up in the house.

His flight was leaving at eight thirty in the morning. By the time, they reached the airport, it was eight o'clock.

"There is no way you'll be able to make this flight," she said to Nick.

"I'll try."

They ran into the terminal and went to the check-in desk. There was nobody there. The flight was closed!!! They went to the Iberia counter and changed his flight for the following day.

"I'm sorry babe, I know you must be upset, but look at the bright side...we get to spend one more day together..."

Nick drove on the way back.

"Can't believe you managed that ride to the airport, babe" he glanced at her, lying on the passenger seat. Her eyes were closing.

"I'm so tired, I can't believe it either. Please drive carefully darling. I don't want to die, not now that I've found you."

She put her hand on his leg, just to make sure he was still there and passed out.

They slept most of the day. It was Carlos, who woke them up. "What, are you still doing here?" He was surprised to see Nick.

"Missed the plane. I'm leaving tomorrow morning."

"Why don't you stay for New Year's Eve?! What's the point flying back just to spend one day in the office? This really doesn't make any sense."

"I have to go back." Nick answered sharply and ended the conversation.

Carlos looked at him, a bit surprised, but didn't say a word.

They went to bed early that night, to make sure Nick got the flight on Wednesday morning.

He woke up at 5.30 am and called a taxi.

"There's no point in you driving me to the airport, honey. You'd be better staying in bed and getting some more sleep."

She was still very tired, so decided not to argue with him about it.

"I'll call you from Madrid."

They held each other for a very long moment.

"I love you!" Nick said.

"I love you too" Isabelle whispered.

"I'll see you next week. I'll pick you up from the airport."

She was flying back to New York the following week, on Thursday.

"I love you Nick, to the moon and back! Please never forget that."

He kissed her one last time.

"I need to go." he said.

And he was gone.

Chapter 26

The next couple of days went slowly.

"I miss him," she confessed to her dad "I feel lonely without him."

"He is a nice guy and a very smart one," Carlos added.

Isabelle was going to Peter's restaurant for New Year's Eve. He was having a big party at his place, and she had nowhere else to go anyway.

Nick was going for dinner with some of his friends in New York and they both had agreed to go back home early and celebrate again together, and once again, next weekend, when she was back in the city.

She arrived at the restaurant at nine o'clock. Peter had put her on his table. She sat at the bar first, to have a quick drink and a chat with Roberto, Peter's partner.

"Señorita, do you have some change to spare, por favor?"

She turned around to see a ten or eleven years old gypsy boy standing next to her.

"How did you get in here?" the question jumped out of her.

Of course, she was surprised to see a gypsy beggar in a

place like this. The kid was holding a white piece of paper in his hands, written on it was 'I have no family. I'm poor. Please give me some money to buy food for me and my little brother. We have nothing to eat.'

She looked at the little boy and felt so sorry for him.

"Let me see what I have for you," she said "Where's my purse?"

It was right there lying on the bar, next to her brand new iPhone. She checked the display... no missed calls.

She had no change in her wallet, all she had were fifty euro bills, but that was a bit too much.

"Get out of here. Who let you in?" Ricardo grabbed the boy and started dragging him out of the restaurant.

"Please don't be so unkind. It's New Year's Eve" Isabelle begged.

She stood up and took the little boy's hand. Peter had heard something was going on and rushed out from the kitchen.

"Pete, he's hungry. Give him some change, please." Isabelle begged again.

"I'll make him something to eat." He said and went back to the kitchen.

Ricardo had released the boy from his grip and the gypsy was standing back next to Isabelle at the bar.

"I don't need a sandwich," he snapped suddenly and started to walk towards the exit.

"As you want" she said in disbelieve.

Peter came out of the kitchen, carrying a piece of bread with ham and cheese.

"Where's the boy?" he asked.

"He left," she said.

He looked at her in shock, then at the bar.

"Where's your iPhone?"

It was gone…together with the poor little hungry boy.

Ricardo ran out after the gypsy but he came back ten minutes later with empty hands.

"He was running like a little devil," his breath was short and there was sweat streaming down his temples. "I knew it! You can never trust a gypsy, but no, you felt soooo sorry for him! Do you think he feels sorry for you now?" he added.

"Oh my God! All my numbers are in that phone. I don't even know Nick's phone by heart, nobody's number actually."

The panic was crowding her. She bit her lips, till the pain brought her back from the shock.

"My car phone! I have a twin card with the same numbers in my car and an old phone at home." Her thoughts were faster than the words from her mouth.

She grabbed her purse to leave.

"I'll be back in a minute," she said to the puzzled Peter and Ricardo.

She got into her car and pressed the redial button on her car phone. The number that came on the display had a 212 area code, so it had to be Nick's. It was ringing.

"Hi honey, I was just about to call you." His cheering voice came through the phone line.

"Thank you, God," she whispered to herself.

She told him briefly what had happened and instead of being upset he just laughed.

"We'll get you a new phone babe. Who cares? It's only important that nothing has happened to you. That's all that

161

matters…I love you! Let me call you back, so your bill won't be that high."

She loved him too. Very much. He made all her problems disappear. No mountain was too high for him, and no sea was too deep. That was her man. She smiled and her heart filled with happiness.

"Five more days and I'll be with you babe," she blew him a kiss.

She went back to the restaurant, but her celebrating mood was gone. She left a little after midnight and went back home. She spent the rest of the night talking to Nick on the phone.

The next day she received an email from Nick that made her cry.

"As I sat down to write this, I thought of all you mean to me. I wouldn't change anything about you. I love you and want you just the way you are. I'm so glad that you are mine, you are everything I have ever hoped for. Every time I think about you, I thank God for you. You bring such joy into my life. When you are afraid, I'll stop your fears, when you are feeling down or discouraged, I will hold you and give you strength again. I am here for you darling. I would not only climb the highest mountain for you, but I would even level the mountains in front of you. I love you enough to die for you." Signed. Nick Walters.

She was flying back to New York, back to her man, on the sixth of January and no one would be stopping her.

Chapter 27

She was watching TV at home and that's when she saw it on the news.

It was a segment on new measures against terrorism in New York. In order to strengthen their security system against terrorism, the United States had provided all the major airports across the country with a new fingerprint scanner, that could read the prints and check the information connected to them in less than five seconds. All the passengers who wanted to enter the United States, had to undergo the fingerprint check. She froze.

"This can't be happening!" she screamed.

Isabelle had been deported from America two years ago for the possession of a fake ID card and a fake drivers license. They had stamped her passport and sent her back to Spain. She was banned from coming back to the States for the period of five years. Thanks to the Visa Waiver program, between the USA and Western Europe, she didn't need a visa to reenter the country, only a genuine passport. So, after she'd returned home, she had declared her passport lost and got a new one. She had been using the new one since then and had never had a problem... Not until now!

If she got fingerprinted, they'd find out that she'd been deported... she started to sweat. She could even serve time in jail for illegal reentry.

"This can't be happening!" she cried out loud.

She was in Spain and Nick was in New York. Her world was collapsing in front of her. She dialed her mom's number.

Isabelle couldn't say a word. The tears were choking her. Her mom heard her weeping on the phone. She'd seen the number on her caller id, so she knew it was Isabelle crying on the other end of the line.

"Calm down. Please calm down and tell me what has happened," her mom pleaded.

"Did you watch the news today?" Isabelle managed to say.

"No, I haven't seen the news yet. Relax and talk to me. First darling, stop crying, because crying will not help in any way."

"They are fingerprinting everyone who wants to enter the USA...and do you remember, I have been deported from there. That means I won't be able to go back for another three years. I'm fucked mom. I can't go back to Nick." She started crying even stronger than before.

"I don't know what to do mom."

She felt so helpless, like she was five years old again and someone had stolen her favorite doll and only her mom could comfort her in that moment.

"Drink some water Isabelle and try to calm down, everything will be all right in the end, I promise you," her mom said.

The next phone call was to Silvia, her sister.

"Call the homeland security office and ask them if everyone needs to be fingerprinted," she begged "Please sis, and I'll call you back in a half an hour."

This was turning into a real disaster. She had all her stuff in Frank's apartment too, but she could not care less about the stuff at the moment!

"I can't imagine my life without Nick anymore, sis!" she cried to Silvia.

"Please call and get this information for me and I'll call you later."

The tears were rolling down her face. The sixth of January was only two days away. Only two days away from being in Nick's arms but suddenly everything was looking very different. The phone rang. She hesitated for a second, but then cleared her throat and answered it.

"Two more days and I will be able to kiss you honey!" Nick's voice was filled with joy and excitement.

"Nick we need to talk. I got something to tell you."

Get straight to it. There was no point fucking around and circling the issue.

"Nick, there might be a problem with me coming back to New York."

"What are you on about? Ha ha, you got me babe. That's funny!" He thought she was only making a joke.

"They won't let me in the country if I get fingerprinted at the airport. I was deported from the USA 2 years ago and I can't come back for another three." He tried to stay cool.

"I'll call you back," he said and hung up.

She didn't hear from him for more than two hours.

"Listen, here's the deal," Nick was back. "You're a Spanish citizen, right? You have a Spanish passport! The homeland security office has released information on the internet, saying they are fingerprinting only people who travel on a visa. You don't need one. There's also a list of the countries who are exempt and Spain is one of them…so you won't be fingerprinted…" he sighed, "I miss you babe, you got me scared. I called my travel agent, and he told me the same…"

"I miss you too," she was still crying.

The house phone rang.

"Stay on the line babe!" she said to Nick and answered it. It was her mom. "Nick, I need to go. Call me later."

"Only if you promise me you'll stop worrying and smile."

"I'll try," she was smiling already.

Her mom repeated more or less the same information that Nick had given her.

"But listen, maybe it will be better if you stay home and don't go back there anymore!"

"I love him mom. I don't want to stay here without Nick."

"It's a big risk you are taking because of him, you know that," her mom said. "He better be good to you and better have serious intentions. Anyway, to avoid any complications, why don't you fly to Canada and ask Nick to come and pick you up from there. They're not that strict on the Canadian border."

"That is a great idea mom. I'll talk to him, and mom, thanks a lot. I am so sorry I got you worried earlier, but I didn't know who else to call."

"That's what moms are for. I love you."

Isabelle called Nick and told him about the conversation with her mom. The idea about Canada wasn't at all bad.

"I have a friend, who lives in Montreal," he said to her.

"You can fly there on Friday, stay with him and I'll drive to Montreal on Saturday to pick you up. We can stay an extra day and drive back to New York on Sunday."

She smiled and realized she could breathe freely again for the first time since she'd watched the news.

"I love you, my super man!"

"Let me check and organize my trip and you can start working on your ticket in the meantime." He put the phone down and sat back in his chair. "Damn, this girl is a piece of work."

On the other side of the world, Isabelle called her travel agent and asked him to book her a flight to Montreal.

"I thought you were flying to New York," the agent said.

"I changed my plans" she said with a smile.

Chapter 28

Isabelle didn't hear from Nick until late that evening.

She was having dinner with Carlos when Nick rang.

"I have a surprise for you Honey Bunny!" he said to her.

"Please don't call me Honey Bunny, you know, it drives me nuts," she said.

"I know, that's why I'm doing it," he laughed.

Nick had spent the entire day working on the Canada project. She deserved a bit of teasing now, the planning had been driving him crazy all afternoon.

"You'll forgive me after you hear this...we are going skiing!" he paused for some more effect and prepared himself for the screams of delight.

He didn't have to wait long. She jumped to her feet, almost turning over the table.

"We are going skiing!" She looked at Carlos. "Dad, we are going skiing in Canada."

She was feeling as excited as a kid in a candy store.

"So do you want to hear the details now?" Nick asked slowly.

"Oh, honey, thank you!...have I told you yet today that I love you?"

"You will fly to Montreal on Thursday. You will be staying overnight with my friend. I've spoken with him already, he knows all about it. I'll finish in the office on Friday, hopefully by midday, and drive up straight away after work. I'll be with you probably by eight in the evening, I'll pick you up and we'll..." he paused again... "Are you ready for this? We'll go on up to Tremblant. I have booked us into Hotel Quintessence for three nights. Friday, Saturday and Sunday, departing on early Monday morning. It's a five star hotel and they have the junior suite overlooking a lake for us. The hotel will organize our ski passes for the three days and I've called a ski rental and have booked all the ski gear we need. Your job will only be to help me pick up a nice ski jacket, because I can't find my old one...oh and one more thing. I really need you to be there and love me, because I have missed you so much Ms. Lucardi."

There were no words to express her feelings at that moment. She loved him more than she ever thought she would be capable of.

"I'll be there!" she said.

"So go home and start packing Honey Bunny! Did you get your ticket today?"

"I was waiting for your call, to know your plan. I have a few options on hold and I will be calling the ticket agency first thing tomorrow morning," she said "so, consider it done."

Chapter 29

Isabelle took the flight via London. It was Mallorca London, London Montréal. Her return flight was booked for three months later, from New York to London. She wanted to spend a week with April on her way back to Spain.

Everything was working out so perfectly. She still couldn't believe she was on her way to skiing in Tremblant. It was as if God had looked into her heart and had made all her wishes come true. It was only a week ago that she'd had a call from her friend Karin, who'd invited her to go skiing with her and her husband in Saint Moritz and she'd had to say no. Then the horror of the last few days…when she thought she'd had lost Nick forever…and now she was on her way to go skiing with him in Canada. It seemed unreal.

She boarded the British Airways aircraft, found her seat and took a sleeping pill. She closed her eyes tight and whispered

"Thank you God."

A few minutes later she was in dreamland.

The plane landed in Montreal on Thursday evening. There were no problems going through customs and immigration.

Isabelle liked the Canadians, all very friendly. It was a different story with their weather. She'd heard that Canada was cold, but she hadn't expected North Pole temperatures.

She was waiting in the line for a taxi when her phone rang, but she couldn't even imagine taking her gloves off or moving the scarf away from her face.

"Whoever this is has got to wait! It's a matter of life and death."

The icy wind was making her eyes fill up with tears but she was anything but sad.

"Why had no one warned me about this? I could've put three pairs of pants and two coats...I could have used a few more scarfs as well."

She couldn't even think properly anymore. It felt like her brain had been frozen too. Finally, she managed to get into a cab, half alive, half frozen and gave the driver the address.

Fernand lived 20 minutes away from the airport, a fancy one bedroom apartment in downtown Montreal.

"Don't worry about it," he'd said when he saw the confused look in her eyes.

"I'll be sleeping on the sofa tonight. You're having the bed." That was so sweet of him, Isabelle thought.

Fernand was twenty two years old, but he looked no older than eighteen. He was quiet in his own way. His face had fine features with shiny black eyes, surrounded by curly black hair.

"Are you hungry?" he asked.

"We could go and grab something to eat. There are a few nice places down the block."

"Going out again, in that cold?" said Isabelle. The thought

alone sent a chill through her body and made her shiver.

The problem was, she was hungry, and she figured that being a young man meant there would for sure be no food in his fridge.

"How far is it?" she asked very carefully. "Can we take a cab?"

He could not help laughing. Her face expression was so full of hope.

"It's only two minutes walk from here" He assured her.

"Oh yeah?" she said disbelievingly and smiled.

They went to a cozy Italian restaurant that was at least ten minutes away. Fernand ordered a bottle of red wine to warm them up. He was such an adorable young man. Isabelle caught herself staring at him a few times and studying his features. There was something very seductive about him whilst still looking so innocent.

Her phone dragged her out of her thoughts.

"Sometimes I feel like I'm working for Telecom as an operator." She sighed. "It must be Nick."

They had already talked several times since she'd landed, but that obviously wasn't good enough.

"What are you guys up to?" Nick asked.

"Fernand dragged me out into the cold again, but he repaid me with a nice bottle of red," she said smiling.

"Be careful with him" Nick said, and she could feel the jealousy in his voice.

"Don't even go there Nick!" she stopped him right away. "We are about to get our food and I will be going straight to bed after this. I've been on the road for more than twenty hours already," she moaned.

"I bet my ass you slept the whole flight to Montreal," he stopped her this time.

"This doesn't count. I was sitting, not lying. And I was worried about all sorts of things."

They both laughed and she promised to call him before she went to bed.

Through dinner, Fernand told her all about the city and it's buzzing nightlife…

"Fancy going to check out one of the clubs after this?"

"You got to be joking. I'm knackered. The only place I might go before bed would be your sofa for a short TV session or a movie. A club…Hell no!"

"That's cool with me. Do you smoke pot?" He looked at her. "I got some good stuff at home."

She remembered the last few times when she attempted to smoke grass and turned red.

"I've done it, but not regularly." She said and looked down at her hands.

"You should try this stuff. It will make you sleep like an angel." They finished their food, drank the wine and went home.

Fernand rolled a joint and put 'Snatch' on the TV. She loved the movie. She had a few puffs and started to feel the jet lag, the wine and the grass taking their toll on her tired body. She fell asleep about a second later.

Fernand looked at her sleeping and smiled.

"Lucky Nick," he thought. "This girl was quite a find.".

He tried to wake her up, after the movie finished, but she didn't move. So he covered her with a blanket and took the bed instead.

The next day they stayed in, ordered a pizza and watched TV. Isabelle was feeling comfortable with him. It surprised her, because normally it took her longer to open up to people but there was something about him she really liked. It was definitely not a sexual attraction, but there was something.

Nick turned up as promised, a few minutes before eight. Fernand went to meet him downstairs, while she went to the bathroom to put on some make up. She was a little confused.

What the hell was going on with her? She loved Nick with all her heart, in every way. He was the perfect match for her.

But Fernand had her feeling confused and she didn't even know anything about him. She didn't even find him sexually attractive…but still she was feeling confused. She looked at herself in the mirror for a long moment.

"This has to be all the stress I've been going through lately or maybe all those MDMA pills we popped over Christmas are still kicking in and messing with my head."

She heard the door open and came out from the bathroom.

He stood there, his arms open, his eyes looking for her. The moment he saw her his face lit up with a bright smile. He took her in his arms, kissed her passionately and all her confusion melted away, like a snowman in the sun. There wasn't even a trace!

She loved Nick Walters. She loved him with all her heart, body and soul. She had missed him so much. She had missed his big strong arms around her that made her feel so safe and secure. And those eyes, those big blue-green eyes with the eyelashes most girls would kill for. Nick Walters was her man.

"Did you have a good time?" he asked her.

"Yes, Fernand has been nice to me, but I am so happy you are here now. Are you tired? You've been on the road for more than seven hours." Isabelle asked him.

"I just need a shot of Tequila and then we should hit the road, if we want to be in Tremblant before midnight."

Fernand rolled a joint and all three of them had a shot. Then half an hour later Nick and Isabelle were in the car on their way to Tremblant.

Chapter 30

They didn't arrive at the hotel till 1.30 am. But even in the middle of the night, Isabelle could see it was beautiful. The whole village sat nestled in-between the slopes. It reminded her of Austria and Arlberg, where she and her family used to spend Christmas, before her mom and dad got divorced. It was all covered in white. Wherever you looked. It was like being in a fairy tale. When she saw their hotel, Isabelle felt like she was the princess and the man next to her, her prince.

The concierge showed them to their room.

It was huge. Breath-taking!

A huge king size bed, a bright sofa, and a enormous man sized fireplace. The bathroom 'area' was the most interesting part of the entire composition. It was a white ceramic vintage bathtub, placed in the middle of the room, to the left of the bed. It seemed that the bathroom, the bedroom, and the living room were all just one big room, as there were no walls to separate them. It looked extraordinary.

"It's amazing honey," Isabelle whispered.

She looked at him and he knew she loved him. He could see it in her eyes. Nick had brought a couple of bottles of her favorite Californian wine, so they ordered some cheese to go with it from room service. It was too late for a big meal, and they wanted to be up early the next day.

He couldn't wait till the next morning to make love to her. Neither could she. They needed each other and they gave each other all the love they had. The miracle of love still existed and they were living proof of it.

Love was not just a story in a book. It was real. It existed. Love was their story.

By the time Isabelle fell asleep in his arms, it was almost 4 am.

He woke her up with kisses a few hours later. The sun was coming through the window, playing on her hair, making it look as if it was made of golden thread. She looked so beautiful...and irresistible. She opened her eyes and smiled at him.

"Good morning, Angel," he said.

"Good morning sweetheart. I want to wake up like this until the end of my days." she replied.

They had breakfast in the small restaurant looking out over the frozen lake at the back of the hotel. She lit a cigarette.

"You got to quit that, now when we're skiing," Nick said.

"You first!" quipped Isabelle. He was smoking just as much as she was.

They finished their coffee and made plans for the day. First on the list was finding a ski outfit for Nick.

They took a walk through the village to the small square, where all the shops were full of people. There was a big crowd on the right side and Isabelle figured out that the ski lift must be there.

There were a few coffee shops and an authentic French looking pancake house. It had 'Crepes' written above it. She took his hand and led him into the first store on their way. He had no idea exactly what they were looking for, but she did. This was her field, she was a professional shopper.

"Where can I find Prada or Bogner?" she asked the sales lady.

"Two stores down on the right. I'm not sure about Prada, but they definitely carry Bogner."

"Thank you very much." She pulled him back towards the exit and he simply followed her.

They found the store they were looking for.

"May I help you?" the assistant asked.

"We want to see your Bogner collection," Isabelle said.

She took them to the far end of the shop and showed them all the ski outfits hanging there.

"Is this is all you have?" Isabelle sighed, disappointed, "these are from five years ago." They left the shop.

The square was filling up with more and more people, all carrying their skis on their shoulders. Everyone was heading towards the lift. It was ten thirty in the morning and it was promising to be a beautiful day.

"Oh, babe, thanks for bringing me here. It's like a fairy tale." She gave him a quick kiss on the chick.

They had to check out three other boutiques till they found the perfect outfit for Nick. The jacket was a combination of dark blue and off-white with loads of pockets, and the cut was perfect. It looked like a regular street jacket, not like those baggy, shapeless ski coats. She'd done a really decent job finding this one. She picked out the matching pants, a pair of gloves and two undershirts. "These are so thin," he touched the undershirts, "are you sure they're going to keep me warm?"

"Don't worry, they will. There's a special thermostatic that's built into the material, that's why they're so expensive."

He looked at the price. "150 dollar a piece…God, are they made of gold?"

"No, they are only light and yet still keep you warm. Same as these socks."

She put them all together and asked the assistant to pack everything.

"Honey, all I need now is your credit card." She was really pleased with her find. It was even better than she had hoped.

They went back to the hotel and got changed. On the way to the lifts, they stopped to pick up their boots and skis. By the time they were sitting in the gondola, it was midday.

It was a beautiful day, still cold, but the sun was shining, covering the slopes with millions of tiny diamonds. She took a deep breath. Skiing was the one and only hobby she had. Despite her amazing figure she didn't do any sports. Isabelle had seen the inside of a fitness studio just twice in her life. She had never jogged or ridden a bicycle. Skiing was her sport. When she was a little girl, her parents used to take her every year for two weeks skiing in Austria. They had spent every Christmas in the mountains of Arlberg. She had never learned how to ski quite like her dad, but she was good enough to go down any slope she wanted.

She and Nick skied for most of the afternoon. Nick was a good skier, so they made a good pair, even in the snow.

They fell and rolled around in the snow, laughed, kissed and cuddled… It was a wonderful day.

They caught the last gondola down at 4 o'clock, then after he'd taken her for a quiet dinner in the evening, they spent the rest of the night making love and lying in each other arms…

The next day went the same way. It was only on Monday that the sun didn't come out.

"You see," said Nick, "we're leaving and the sun refuses to come out. I bet the mountain will miss us," they were still lying in bed. "I wish we could stay longer, but I need to be back in the office tomorrow."

"I know honey. We'll come back next year," she gave him a playful kiss on the nose, "…and the year after that."

"If there is enough snow in New York, we can drive to Vermont one weekend. They've got surprisingly good slopes there too," Nick added.

They packed their bags and checked out of the hotel. She felt a sadness in her heart. It was their first vacation together and it was over.

Chapter 31

The way back to New York was long. It took them about four hours to get to the border. She showed her passport to the patrol officer.

"Where are you going to ma'am?" he asked.

"New York," answered Isabelle.

"What are you going to do there?" he asked next.

"Make love to my boyfriend...day and night!" she thought, but instead she said "I'm going to spend some time with my fiancée."

"Is that you, sir?" the officer asked turning to Nick.

"That is correct." Nick answered.

"Have a pleasant stay," the officer said and handed back her passport.

"That was quite easy," Nick said and gave her a kiss.

She smiled and snuggled against his arm.

They stopped only once, to have something to eat in Abby's and Nick managed to get them back to New York by midnight. The minute Isabelle entered his apartment, she felt like coming back home. It was almost the same feeling she had when she came home to Mallorca.

The next day Isabelle went back to One Sutton Place and life took on it's usual march.

Frank wasn't coming back till Monday the following week. She unpacked, took a shower, and lay down on the couch.

"Welcome back to reality!" she whispered to herself, "Gosh, I'm so not in the mood to go to work tonight and dealing with all these drunk men! Oh…who said life is easy!!"

Chapter 32

The plan was to go to work every night, make lots of money and by Friday be able to chill and enjoy the weekend with Nick. If she did not go to work and therefore made no money, she'd be miserable and her guilt would torture her all through the weekend.

She was missing Nick. She got used to being around him the whole 24 hours in a day and now she was feeling lonely without him. It was like half of her had been taken away. She called her sister.

"Hi sis, how are you?" Isabelle chirped.

"Are you back in NY ? You were supposed to call me last night. I was worried silly about you and both your phones were switched off!" Silvia chided.

"Hey, hey, relax Dr. Watson" Isabelle interrupted her quickly "I'm back in NY and I'm ok, only feeling a bit down."

"Why, has Nick upset you?"

"No, I just miss him sis…We've been together every second of the day for the last week and I feel so empty without him." The sadness was crawling all over her now. "It was so nice being together all the time now he is gone. I felt like I become a part of him, and he'd become a part of me and now he is gone…" Isabelle wailed.

"He is not gone, he's at work, same place you should be going too, if you want to be able to pay Gary his money back, before he kicks your ass, so stop this crap please." scolded Silvia.

Her sister had always been short on emotions. She couldn't remember her being sentimental even. She was always dry, practical and she had always right.

"Of course I'm going to work tonight, I was only feeling a bit sad, that's all. Nothing to worry about," and hung up.

There was a new message showing on the display.

"I miss you more, than words can say," a very timely and welcome message from Nick.

It was around seven that evening when she went to 'Scores'. The club was empty.

"What has happened in here?" she asked. "Did somebody throw a bomb?"

"It's January!" Willow replied. "It's always like this in January."

"Well, this is exactly what I need to hear to brighten my day" Isabelle said crossly.

There were no more than twenty girls working that night. Normally, there should've been between fifty or sixty girls dancing around.

"Whatever! You never know what the night might bring. It could even be a lucky one for me."

Willow laughed, as there was literally no one in the club.

"At least I don't have to deal with the regular drunks on my first night back," she thought, while she was getting dressed. She fixed her hair, put on her make up and went to look for Gaby. She wasn't there either.

"This is getting better by the second." she continued sarcastically. She sat at the bar and said to Willow, "Give me a strong Cosmo please."

It had to be a few hours later, when the first customer came in. Was he lost? He looked like a truck driver with his worn-out jeans, white t-shirt under his open shirt and a baseball cap with "I Love NY" on it. He sat next to Isabelle and ordered himself a diet coke.

"What the fuck is wrong with the world today?" she cried out looking at Willow, the bartender. They both laughed.

The guy's name was Andrew and he was waiting for a friend. He got Isabelle another drink and they started a small talk conversation. Andrew was half American, half Arab. His mom was from Upstate New York and his dad was from Saudi Arabia.

"That's an interesting combination" Isabelle commented." What was someone from Saudi Arabia doing in Upstate New York?!"

They chatted for a while till his friend arrived. He was a handsome looking man in his late thirties. He had black hair and dark eyes. His body was strong and well trained. Isabelle stood up from her chair to introduce herself and found that he wasn't much taller than her.

"My name is Jordan" said Isabelle.

"Joe Brown," he said. "Is that your real name or is it your stage name?" Joe asked.

"It's my name," she said "I'm Jordan. Where are you from Joe?" she asked, swiftly changing the subject.

"Manhattan." Another short answer.

He got himself a vodka on the rocks and drank the whole thing almost down in one. Jordan looked at him in disbelieve.

"Were you thirsty?"

"Willow!" he called to the bartender "give everyone another drink, whatever they've been drinking and get yourself one too. All on me."

It seemed Joe was well known here but it was the first time Isabelle had met him. She must ask Willow about him, she thought to herself. They made a toast and Joe drank his second vodka straight down too.

"He's got to be on something," Isabelle thought. "He must be on coke."

She was checking him out, up and down.

"Why are you looking at me that way?" he caught her staring at him.

"I like you" she said. "You're cool and seem to be lots of fun."

"I'm always fun," he said, then turned around and blew his nose.

"I knew it!" thought Isabelle, "he is on coke!"

There was no doubt about it. His behavior. The way he was talking, the paranoid look in his eyes…

"I better get him out of here and get him into one of the private rooms before someone else does." She thought and stood up from her chair, putting her arms around him. "Do you want to go for a dance Joe?" she whispered in a sexy voice next to his ear, touching it gently with her lips.

"I don't do dances. Not my thing." He snapped back.

"Damn, he's a piece of work," she thought but smiled and pressed her body even harder against his. This was difficult for him to resist.

He put his arms around her waist, "What was your name again?" he said.

"Jordan! I cannot believe you forgot it already, Mr. Joe Brown." She came in even closer to him. Her breasts pressed up against him.

"Do you want another drink, Jordan?"

"Only if you drink with me," she said, putting on her most seductive smile.

"Willow, another round for everyone!" he said without taking his eyes off Jordan's body. Andrew was still sitting on the bar, next to them.

"Go find yourself a girl, buddy," Joe said to him "Put it all on my bill and let's move to the back!"

"Why don't we go to the back room now and wait for them there," Jordan suggested.

Joe finished his third drink in one go.

"This man is a trip," she thought.

He threw a fifty dollar bill on the bar and took her hand.

"Willow, call the private room host for me please... my darling!"

"Are you going in there this soon Joe?" Willow cried out and Jordan had the burning desire to strangle her. "Don't leave me here all by myself."

"What the fuck is she trying to do? Ruin my night?" thought Jordan, looking at her angrily, but Willow wouldn't give up.

"Don't you want a shot?"

"Send it to the room, girl. Where is that host...is he coming from New Jersey now or what?!"

A guy in a tuxedo showed up at that moment and shook Joe's hand.

"Nice to see you again, Mr. Brown. How are you tonight...I see you already got a beautiful lady at your side."

"I'm fine, thanks and I'll be even better once you put me in one of those rooms at the back, so let's move my man."

They followed the tuxedoed man to a door which he opened with a card key.

"After you," he said and let Jordan and Joe to go first.

There were two small coffee tables surrounded by black leather couches. A flat screen TV on the wall was showing a boxing match live from Las Vegas with the sound down. Isabelle remembered that 'Scores' was actually a Sports bar and Cabaret. The light was dimmed in the room, so your eyes had to adjust to it.

"Bring us a bottle of Dom and some candles...can't see my girl in this darkness here."

The Tuxedo disappeared.

It was silent in the room. She could hear Joe breathing and could feel his eyes fixed on her as if he was undressing her with his eyes. Touching or any kind of body contact was not allowed in 'Scores', so she didn't have to worry about him falling all over her, but there was definitely a tension in the air.

"So..." she tried to break the silence... "do you smoke? I think I left my cigarettes on the bar."

"I'll ask the waiter to bring a pack of Marlboro with the drinks...I fancy one too." He lay back on the couch and put his hand on her leg. "You're a real sweetheart, you know that?! Where're you from? Don't remember seeing you here before."

"I was born in Barcelona but live in Mallorca. You might not know where that is but…"

"Of course I do. I was in Ibiza a few years ago and went to Mallorca on my boat for the day."

"Now we are talking, "she thought "He's playing in the first Liga!"

She knew lots about boats and big yachts, so now the conversation was saved.

"What boat do you have?"

"Oh, that one in Ibiza was chartered. It was a Princess 65. It's a beautiful boat."

"It's a wonderful boat." She knew exactly which one he meant. It was an almost seventy foot boat with a flybridge.

"Did you drive it on your own or did you need a skipper?"

"I used a captain because I'm not that good at parking it. Also, if you travel around on it, you don't get a mooring every time and if we ended up having to anchor outside the port, you need someone to stay on the boat and look after it while you're out for dinner."

"I hear you, I know what you mean, babe." she said.

The waiter came in with a bottle of champagne and a plate of strawberries.

"With compliments from the kitchen for you, Mr. Brown!"

"You seem to be famous here Mr. Brown. How come I've never seen you before?" She picked out a strawberry and let him have a taste.

"I've never seen you either, but better late than never." He ran his fingers through her hair. It felt silky smooth.

"Would you like something else sir?" the waiter asked.

"Yeah, bring us two packs of Marlboro light…and listen, my friend is out there, the one with the baseball cap on. Send him in if you see him." He turned back to Isabelle and fixed his eyes on hers.

"I forgot where we were! Ah yes, boats! So, the Princess 65 was chartered, but I have a boat down in Palm Beach. A Sunseeker. I bought it in England a year ago. Went to that boat show in…oh, I can't remember the name!"

"Southampton, I was there twice. Not so special, though. If you are really into boats, you should check out the one in Düsseldorf. It's the biggest boat show in Europe."

"Girl, you are scary. Where did you learn all that stuff?"

"I just love boats." She smiled "And I live on an island."

"Cheers!" he raised his glass. "You're quite interesting to talk to. You are an incredibly beautiful girl as well. Don't get me wrong, but most of the girls in here are plain and simple. I'm glad I met you."

"You mean, you're glad you stole me away from your friend. I was talking to Andrew first, remember?"

"Andrew is my limo driver. He's here because of me, but if you miss him, don't worry, he'll be here any minute." She burst out laughing.

"I wasn't far from the truth then. When first I saw him I thought he was a truck driver."

He laughed too. The door opened and Andrew came in.

"Speak of the Devil!" Joe looked at him. "Where's your girl?"

"She's getting something to eat at the bar and I'll bring her in afterwards. Why? Do you need something?"

They started whispering and Jordan couldn't hear what they were saying, but she could guess what it was about. Drugs! She saw Andrew take something out of his pocket and slide it into Joe's hand. She looked the other way and said nothing.

"So, I'll come back, when my girl's finished her food." Andrew said.

"Ok. Don't be long," Joe replied.

Andrew disappeared back into the restaurant. It was just the two of them in the room again.

"I'm sorry, I need to take care of something." Joe said "I need to go to the bathroom but I'll be right back."

He stood up to go when she stopped him.

"You don't need to go to the bathroom to take a line. Plus, I want one too."

He looked shocked at the first. He didn't know what to say... should he deny it?

"What the fuck," he thought and pulled out the packet that Andrew had given him from his pocket. He tapped out some of the powder onto the table and made two big lines with his credit card.

"Do you have a dollar bill?" she asked.

"Only poor people sniff out of a dollar bill," he said and pulled out a hundred dollar note.

She rolled it tightly until it looked like a tiny straw and handed back to him.

"No, ladies first!" and gave it back to her.

"Can you hold back my hair?" she asked and leaned in towards the table and snorted up the powder... "oh it's good... and strong." she commented.

He took the bill and sniffed his line.

"Yeah, not bad! Cheers to new friends and lots of fun." he said.

"Cheers!" she raised her champagne glass up to his. "Shall we do some shots?" she added.

"Of course. The night is young, and we are just starting." he agreed.

"They still haven't brought us any cigarettes," she said "I'll go get some, because I don't know about you, but I need to smoke when I do coke."

"So do I. Dying for one now." Joe added.

"I'll be right back." She left the room… "I better hurry up cause he'll freak out there by himself," she thought to herself.

She went to the bar and ordered four shots and two packs of Marlboro.

"Put it on Joe Brown's bill" she said to Willow, the bartender, "By the way, what was wrong with you earlier? Why were you trying to keep him in here?"

"I need to make money as well." Willow said "…and he is always so generous with the tips."

"I'll make sure he gives you a tip before he leaves, but don't do that to me again, please." Jordan said.

"Cool! I'll send the waiter with your order as soon as I see him babe. Sorry for before." Willow replied.

"In the meantime, can I have two of your cigarettes, Willow…I promised Joe, I'd come back with a smoke for him."

"Don't forget your promise to me though!" she said and gave her two cigarettes.

Jordan ran back to the room and found Joe at the door.

"Where are you going?" said Jordan.

"To look for you." Joe replied.

"Oh babe, did you get bored without me?" she asked.

"Yes, I did," he said.

He was so sweet. They went back inside and she lit a cigarette.

"This one is for you." She put it between his lips.

"So, what brought you to N.Y.?" he asked.

"Dancing." she replied.

"Can't you dance in Spain?"

"Not really…" she said, "Sure, there are plenty of clubs in Europe. I've never been in any of them, but I have heard from different people, that a strip club is more or less the same as a brothel. First of all, the girls are totally nude, and secondly, they don't really have any rules over there. That means a man can touch you anywhere they want and most of the girls prostitute themselves. So, I never actually thought about even trying it over there. Besides, if you can have real sex for the same amount of money, why would you spend it just to see someone's tits?"

"You're right. It makes sense what you are saying. How long have you been dancing?" he asked.

"It's been four months now. I came to N.Y. in the beginning of September."

"Oh, so you're still new to this business then!""…and I don't have any intention of growing old in it either!" She added. "I want to dance for another couple of months and then start doing something else."

"Why dance another couple of months? Why not stop right now?" he asked.

"I owe some money." was her simple answer.

"Ahh, not the same old stripper story, please." he rolled his eyes. "That's the truth! I'm not lying and you're mean!" she retorted.

He took a deep drag out of his cigarette and put it out.

"That's the same story all the girls say here. Either they owe money, or they are putting themselves through school. It's all the same."

"Whatever you say, but why ask me, if you don't believe me?" "You're right…do you want another line?" He smiled at her.

"Is the Pope catholic?" she answered.

They were really enjoying each other's company.

The bottle of champagne was almost done by the time Andrew came back in with a short, dark haired girl.

"Hi everybody, my name is Sky." she giggled.

"This is Jordan and that's Joe." Andrew introduced the rest of the group. "A glass of champagne?" "Yes please honey," she giggled again.

They sat down on the couch next to Joe.

"Are you ready for your dance now sweetie?" Sky asked.

Andrew put his hands behind his head and lay back, spreading his legs, so she could give him a proper lap dance.

Sky was good. Her body was like a model's, but she had big breasts and a nice butt. Her hips moved very sexily in time with the music.

"Do you want her to dance for you?" Joe turned to Isabelle.

"No thanks. I'm not into girls…I like guys…100 percent straight."

"Have you never been with another woman?" he asked.

"Yeah, for lunch or shopping!" was her reply.

They both laughed. He liked her dry British humor. It was different to the usual. She was refreshing, in general, he thought. He had come to look for another girl, but she hadn't been there…and he had not expected to meet someone like Jordan, in this place.

He'd been seeing one of the girls here for the last three months. He just wanted to say hello to her. When he found out that Georgina wasn't working this evening, all he wanted was to have a drink at the bar and let Andrew take him home after that. That was his plan, two and a half hours ago…now he had a brand new one. How could he make Jordan to come to his house?

"What are you doing after work?" he asked carefully.

"Going home, taking a sleeping pill and trying to sleep." she replied.

"Do you live far away from here?" he asked.

"Across the street. One Sutton Place," she said.

"Oh, really. That's great. I have a place downtown at 75th and 1st. It looks like we live pretty close to each other," he pointed out.

"Yes, we do," she agreed.

He didn't dare to ask her right then if she'd come back with him. So he decided to ask her just before he leaves and then ask Andrew to pick her up from her place.

"Joe, can I get some of that stuff I gave you?" Andrew asked. "My girl here is getting tired and sleepy."

"Coffee time" Joe said and pulled the coke out from his pocket again. This time he made three lines.

"What about Andrew?"

"He doesn't drink, doesn't smoke, doesn't do drugs," Joe answered.

"What...is he a saint, or what?"

"No, just a limo driver, but he does screw everything that walks his way and wears a skirt."

"That's not true!" Andrew protested, while everyone was having a laugh at his cost. "Sky is coming with us later." he said, trying to change the subject.

"Where are you all going?" Jordan asked.

"Back to Joe's place. We want to party some more, and this place is closing in an hour. Do you want to come?" Andrew asked.

Oh oh! She didn't know what to say. She still hadn´t been paid for the time she had been in the room, which was 1500 dollars and she hoped Joe would give her another 500 dollars, because he liked her. She didn't want to spoil her chances of getting this money by saying "No", but equally she didn't want to say "Yes" and not show up after. She didn't want to make him think she was a liar, because she wanted to keep him as a client. One thing was sure though, she wasn't going anywhere after work.

Isabelle didn't want to get into trouble with Nick. Oh God, if she didn't answer his phone call after 12 midday, he'll freak out, like he did the last time...and if she goes to Joe's, there would be no way she would go to bed before 7 am. No way... she knew herself!!!

"I'll think about it," she said and lay back to put her head on Joe's shoulder. "Do you want me to come babe?" she whispered with her sexy voice in his ear.

A heat wave went all through his body.

"I would love you to come…we'll have a few lines and a couple of drinks…and I'll let Andrew drop you off at yours after that. I really do like you, and I want to get to know you better," he said.

"So do I," she lied. That was her job. What could she do? That's why she was there…to make men feel comfortable and feel good about themselves. That's why she was getting paid.

"Do you have your phone with you? Take my number down and give me a call when you get out of here. Send me the exact address and me and Sky will take a cab to your place." He typed in her number in his phone.

"Is that right one, or is it a fake one?" he asked.

"You don't believe me about anything, do you? Why don't you dial it and listen to my mailbox. You can even leave me a nice message if you want."

He did that. Now she had his number. She could always call him later with an excuse and go home to sleep. Everything was working out perfectly… The VIP host came into the room.

"How is everybody? I hope you are all having a fun time." He shook Joe's hand. "Nice to see you again Joe. It's been a while."

"Yeah, I was in Florida over Christmas. Just came back to the city last Saturday."

"Would you like something else from the bar because it's 3.30 am and it's the last call for alcohol? So, if you all want something, now is your last chance."

"Get us a round of shots then and close the bill." Joe said.

"What are we doing about the girls?" the host asked.

Joe pulled out one of his credit cards.

"Put the girl's money on that one. What do we have... Jordan has been here for three hours and Sky for an hour. Make it 2,500 dollars."

The host disappeared and came back a few minutes later with a stack of monopoly money. The girls were getting paid in 'funny money' symbolically and the day after, they could exchange their 'funny money' for a check in the office with an additional charge of 10 percent commission. Joe gave Jordan 2000 of it and the rest to Sky.

"I hope you are happy with this?" he said to Isabelle.

"Of course, I am. Thanks, honey."

The waiter brought the bar bill and the shots. Joe signed it.

"Don't forget to tip Willow. She's my friend." Isabelle piped up.

He put a fifty dollar bill on the tray.

"So, are you coming?" Joe asked.

"Yes, I am. Give me a call when you're at your place. I'm gonna get changed now, so I can get out of here as soon as possible." replied Isabelle.

They all knocked back their shots and returned to the bar area.

"Thank you very much for the good time, guys." Isabelle said. She gave Joe a kiss. "I will see you later," she whispered before she turned around and left for the dressing room.

Sky was so excited.

"Oh my God, we did pretty well tonight, considering there were no customers here, besides Andrew and Joe," she was giggling all the way to the dressing room. "Did you get the address? Andrew said we are taking a taxi together. Oh, I am so happy. Can't believe he gave me all this money...I was there no longer than 40 minutes and danced two or three times."

She was getting on Isabelle's nerves and she was a problem too. Now Isabelle had to look for an excuse in front of her as well for not coming and make her believe it.

"I must go to the bathroom. I think I am getting my period. I'm not supposed to but it feels like it." Isabelle laid the groundwork.

She went to the bathroom and smoked a cigarette in there.

"Yes, I got it," she said to Sky back in the dressing room. "I don't have any tampons and it's really heavy. It's probably because of the drugs and the alcohol. Uhh!" she pretended being angry. "What am I supposed to do now? I can't call Joe and tell him…hi honey, I just got my period…oh, that's really fucked up man. Sky, do you have any ideas darling?"

"I don't know…" Sky was getting confused. "I guess you should go home and get some rest and we can tell Joe that the manager kept us here, because he found out that we'd been doing drugs in the room. We managed to talk our way out of it, but by the time he had let us go, it was far too late to go to his place. Call him in twenty minutes and say you are calling him from the bathroom, just to let him know about the situation. And don't forget to tell him we are sorry and we hope to see them soon." Isabelle stared at Sky in disbelieve.

"Girl, you just blew my mind. Has anybody ever told you, that you are the most brilliant liar in the whole world? That was good. The only thing is, you need to repeat it again, so I can remember it. You see, I am blond, that means I am slow." They both laughed.

It was 4.30 am when they left the club. Isabelle called Joe and told him the story Sky had invented. It all went ok.

She was standing at the traffic light now and her mind went to her man, Nick. She dialed his number.

"Hi honey," his sleepy voice came through the phone line. Her heart melted when she heard him.

"I miss you honey. Can I come sleep in your house?" She asked.

"Of course. I had hoped you'd say that and have left the door open."

She got in a cab.

Chapter 33

Isabelle woke up at 10.30 the next morning, to the sound of her cell phone ringing. She wondered who could be calling her at this time.

"Hello…are you sleeping?" It was Joe. His voice was husky and he sounded a little bit drunk still.

"Yes, I was." She answered. "Did you just wake up?"

"I've haven't been to sleep yet. What are you up to?… ah…do you want to come around to my place? We're still partying. Andrew can come and pick you up."

"Oh babe, I'm still in bed, I still need a few more hours sleep. You know what time we went to bed last night?! It was early this morning…I need some more sleep." Her voice sounded really tired. "And I can't start drinking and sniffing now, I need to work tonight."

"Don't worry about working. I'll take care of you. You're not going to work tonight." he said.

"What do you mean?" she asked.

"Exactly what I am saying. I will take care of you. I'll write you a check for the work you miss," he clarified.

She paused on the phone. Now that was a different story. She knew he was generous and would write her a check for at least 1000 dollars…and if she goes to work, she might make no money at all. She checked the time,10.45 am. Nick would be back there by midday. What was she supposed to do about him? He won't be very happy about this idea.

"I'm sorry babe, I can't," and hung up…she couldn't believe her own words. She just blown away 1000 bucks, so she could be at home when her man comes home for ten minutes to say "good morning" to her and give her a kiss.

"Great!" she thought "I'm completely losing my mind lately. That was 1,000 bucks or maybe even 2,000!!"

She looked at her phone, tempted to call Joe back and tell him she'd changed her mind and she would be coming. Instead, she pulled the duvet over her face and tried to think about something else. Love, sex, kisses, Nick…anything, but drugs and money.

Nick came back from the office at exactly 12 am. She had taken her shower and was lying on the couch, drinking a coffee.

"You're awake already." He was holding a latte in his hand. "This is for you honey," he sat next to her and gave her a kiss.

She wasn't in the best of moods. She hated herself. On the one hand, she couldn't betray Nick's trust and run off to Joe's party, on the other, she resented Nick for stopping her going. She really needed the money. Poor guy, he didn't even know what he'd done wrong and there he was sitting next to her with a latte. She took a sip.

"Did you put any sugar in it?" she asked.

"I didn't know how many you want."

"You don't know, how I take my coffee, after all this time?" she exclaimed.

She was looking for a fight, she couldn't help it. She didn't want to take it out on him, but the frustration was overwhelming her.

"What's wrong with you today?" Nick asked, "Do you want me to leave you alone?"

"No babe, I'm sorry. Nothing to do with you. I'm just in a bad mood. I had nightmares all night long and my phone hasn't stopped ringing the whole morning, so I'm tired and grumpy."

She touched his face gently. It really wasn't his fault that she was confused about her decision and couldn't make up her mind. He was trying his best and he'd always been so patient with her. It wasn't fair to make him suffer because of her own insecurity. She should be more honest with him and talk to him about everything. She should've told him about going to London with Frank in the first place, but she hadn't. Why? Because she was scared. She wasn't doing anything wrong. She wasn't having sex or anything of the sort, but she knew that he wouldn't understand. And now it was the same situation with Joe Brown. God was she angry. She could have just gone to his place, stayed for a couple of hours, had a few drinks with him and his friend, taken her check and left, and then had dinner with Nick tonight. Instead, she had to go to work and wait at the empty bar till 4 am. The anger was boiling up inside her.

Nick was still sitting on the couch next to her, stroking her hair.

"Didn't you have a good night yesterday? You know, if you are worried about money and if you are behind with your payments, I can help you. I could lend you the money and when business picks up again in February, you can pay me back." he suggested kindly.

His eyes were so big and so green. He was so handsome, sitting there in his black suit and perfect white shirt. So pure and innocent. She tried to imagine Joe who hadn't slept all night, still wearing the same clothes from the night before. The smell of smoke and alcohol would be filling the room. That thought alone made her shiver.

"I love you sweetie, you are so nice to me. Sometimes I think you deserve a lot better than me." She really meant it.

"I don't want anyone else but you. You are everything I ever wanted. And if you are in a bad mood today, it's alright. Everyone has bad days. I know what will make you feel better…" he said.

She could hear the enthusiasm growing in his voice.

"Sex?" she said.

"That too, but I was actually thinking of giving you one of the guest passes I have from my gym and sending you there for an hour. You will feel brand new after. They have a steam room and a sauna. It will take away your hangover and clean your lungs from the smoke. It's not far from here. You can walk down to it. It's on the 3rd avenue and 52nd street."

It sounded good, but she knew she wouldn't ever do it. Isabelle had never been into training and working out. The sauna sounded good, but she'd already washed and blow dried her hair, so there was no chance of her spending the afternoon in the gym.

"No thanks babe. I think I'll just get in a cab and go back to my place, eat something and try to get some more sleep, before I go to work."

"If that's what you want. I only want to see you feel better honey," he smiled "and stop picking on me."

She laughed, she had to. He was so sweet.

"You are the best man under the sun. Do I tell you this hundred times a day? I'm sorry, but I need to say it one more time. You, Nicholas Walters, are the best man in this world, and I am the happiest woman being your girlfriend."

To hell with Joe and his offer. She couldn't risk what she had here for a thousand bucks, not even for a million. She pushed herself up from the sofa and pursed her lips asking for a kiss. She didn't have to wait long till she felt his lips touching hers and covering her face with hot passionate kisses. He knew how to touch her, not to hurry or push her in any way that would make her feel uncomfortable. She needed him now. She needed him right now. And he wanted all of her.

Her long, gentle fingers were undressing him, helping him out of his jacket and unbuttoning his shirt. She read the promise in his soft green gaze. He read the need, the fear and the desire in hers. He wanted to spend the rest of his life exploring every inch of her body and her mind, until she understood that he was born to be her lover and no one else. That he was the only one who could give her the pleasure she deserved.

She gave a gentle moan. He lowered himself, so very gently at first and then hard and possessively. He took her right there on the couch. He thrust himself into her, into the deepest part of her. She was responding to his every move, every touch, every kiss. He made her want him so much, made her crave his body.

She could hear her own moaning…such pleasure, her body out of control and his voice in her ear whispering "I love you, I love you so much."

He was kissing her wildly, he couldn't get enough of her. He tried to absorb all the pleasure they were feeling. He took her with him into the world of ecstasy. She pulled him tight to her and he reached even deeper into her, just to feel her climax.

"Come with me" she whispered, "come with me babe."

He couldn't stop himself any more, he couldn't stop that feeling lifting him to the top of his pleasure and letting him collapse on the top of her. He cuddled her in his arms.

"I love you honey, more than you know." She murmured, her lips close to his ear. She felt so happy, lying there, safe in his arms.

"I have to go." He broke the idyllic dream. "I'm sorry honey, but I really have to go."

He jumped in the shower.

"What time do you finish tonight?" she asked.

"Around 9 pm. Why?"

"I don't know. I don't feel like working tonight and if I still feel this way later, I might call off for tonight."

"That would be great! Just remember, I don't want you to drive yourself crazy over money. Promise me you'll tell me if you're late with your payments, so I can help you." "I promise," she said.

He got dressed quickly, kissed her and left. She laid on the sofa and turned the TV on to channel 7. It was time for 'All my children'. Isabelle loved soap operas. As she was working at night time she never had a chance to watch any movies. She watched all the daytime shows like 'All my children', 'One life to live' and her favorite, which was 'General Hospital'.

She felt a lot better. Sex was really the best stress reliever.

It was almost 3 pm when Joe called her again.

"Don't tell me, you are still parting" she laughed.

"Yes I am. I have a few friends over here with me, but I miss your company. So, I thought, you'd be done sleeping by now and you might decide to pop in and say hello." Now was her chance.

"Joe, I need to work tonight babe, I really can't" she paused and let him take the lead again.

"I told you don't worry about your work. It's done. I got your check written already, waiting here for you."

"You are joking, aren't you?" she said, knowing he wasn't.

"Why don't you jump in a taxi and come over...or better still, tell me where you are and I'll send Andrew to pick you up." "I'll take a taxi," she quickly replied.

She didn't want to be seen by the doorman downstairs, leaving the building in a limousine.

"How long do you need to get here?" he was really desperate.

"20 minutes" she said.

"Ok. Great! The address is 70th and 1st avenue, 366 east 70th street. Call me when you are in the building and I'll send someone to get you."

She put the phone down. "Oh my God, what am I doing?" She got dressed quickly and left the apartment.

Chapter 34

It wasn't even 10 minutes later when she was standing in front of a building with a sign '366 east 70th street' on it. She called Joe's number.

"I'm downstairs." she said.

"Right. I'm coming to get you." he answered.

He showed up a few minutes later, unshaven, still wearing the black shirt and the black jeans, from the night before, no shoes and smelling of alcohol, exactly as she had predicted.

"I can't believe you've not been to bed." she said.

"There are no memories from sleeping." was his reply.

He took her to the 40th floor and opened his apartment door.

"Come in, I need to introduce you to the rest of my guests."

There were three more people in there. Andrew, another man, and a young girl.

"That's Tom and Jacqueline" he nodded to the couple. "You've met Andrew already."

"Hi everybody. Sorry for joining the party this late," she said. "Hey there, we've been dying to meet you. Joe has been

talking about you all the night long. Now I can see why."
Tom said "Do you want something to drink? We have wine,
beer, whisky, or vodka."

"I guess I have a lot to catch up, so I'll take vodka…
vodka lemon."

Jacqueline went in the kitchen and start making
her a drink.

"Jordan, do you want it strong or light?"

"Light, thank you. By the way, my name is Isabelle. I use
Jordan only as a stage name at work."

"Oh, I like Isabelle." Joe said. "Why didn't you tell me
your real name yesterday?"

"I needed to get to know you better. I'm telling it to you
now, though. Everything comes when the time is right.
So this is where you live…" she almost stumbled over her
words…This really wasn't what she was expecting to see! It
was a large studio, with an old cheap kitchen, worn out grey
carpet, a cheap couch with a wooden table in front of it and
a double bed. There was a TV and a stereo. That was it, that
was all the furniture in the apartment.

"No, but I own this place and I use it for parties and
stuff…I have a house in Long Island, where I live with my
wife and kids, but when I come to the city, I always stop here."

She didn't like the place, but actually, it wasn't any of
her concern.

"I'll stay till 8 or 9 o'clock and I guess by that time, they'll
be falling asleep," she thought to herself. "If they've been up
all night they've got to get tired at some point, no matter how
much coke they've sniffed. Then I'll go home, take a shower
and go to see Nick."

She sipped on her vodka. Sounded like a cool plan, she thought.

There was a big pack of coke on the table and Tom started to make lines for everyone.

"I'll just pretend, I'm taking it and will blow it onto the floor" she thought, watching him snort his line.

"Are you trying to kill us?" she asked Tom. "This is almost half a gram per line. I can't do that much. Give me that card." She reached for his credit card. "I'll do it myself."

He passed the card and watched closely at what was she doing, as if he had read her mind. Seemed like she had no choice. She sniffed the white powder and gave him back his 100 dollar bill.

"So, you're working in 'Scores'?" Jackie said. "I was used to work there years ago, but then I met Tom and he didn't like the idea of me dancing there anymore."

"Well, I'm not planning on dancing there for years, it's more of a temporary situation." Isabelle explained.

"Do you have a boyfriend?" Jackie asked.

Everybody's eyes were fixed on her. That was a very tricky question.

"I am dating." She answered.

"This was a smart answer." Joe laughed. "I told you she's a smart girl. She's not only beautiful, but she has a head on her shoulders as well."

They realized they wouldn't get any precise answers from their interrogation, so they let it be and returned to the cocaine and their drinks.

Tom had a limo company. That's where Andrew came from. Jackie was his girlfriend and she wasn't doing anything.

Joe? She still had no idea what was he doing for a living. He never talked about himself.

"What about you Mr. Mystery man?" she tried to sound easy. "How do you make your money?"

"I rob banks…seriously. Not in the literal meaning of the word, but close to it. I am an investor. I invest and supervise the money from other people. My family has been in this business for many years, so I just took after my dad, as he did after his dad, etc."

"This is very exciting. So, you work with money every day." Isabelle said.

"Yes, same as you. We all do it for the money or are you going to work because you're bored?"

That was a good question. Of course, she was doing it for the money, but on the other hand, she didn't plan on working her whole life, just for the money. One day, when she starts her own fashion business and starts designing clothes, she won't be doing it just for the money. Oh no, she will be doing that with all her passion. Of course, she would hope to get paid back for it, but she would not be doing it only for the money.

They were having a fun time. Joe was a very smart guy and lots of fun to talk to. She was doing line after line with all the rest of the group and she couldn't stop talking. She didn't notice the time passing, but she almost screamed, when she noticed it was 7.30 pm. She was in trouble. There were six missed calls on her phone. She had forgotten that it was on silent. Nick had been trying to reach her and he would be angry by now.

"Joe, I have to go back to my place for a half an hour," she said. "I need to check up on my room mate," she lied, but no one seemed to notice.

"Take Andrew with you. He'll wait in the car." Joe said, "And don't even think about going to work babe, you are staying here with me."

And just to confirm how serious he was, he reached for his wallet and pulled a check out of it.

"This is for you, but you have to promise me, that you are coming back."

She looked at the numbers and could barely hide her surprise. Sure, was she coming back. Why should she go to the club, waiting for the next victim to come, when she was holding a check for 2,000 dollars in her hand? She had done pretty well the last few days. She smiled and gave him a kiss on the cheek.

"Thank you, babe. I promise, I won't be long. Half an hour at most."

She took her bag and left together with Andrew. The first thing she did when they were in the car, was to check her voice mail. There were five messages. Four from Nick and one from Frank, telling her, he would be back in N.Y. on Sunday night. Nick didn't sound too happy, but also not too bad. He thought that she was sleeping. Taking a nap, before work. That's all.

She left Andrew, waiting in the car in front of her building. She needed two things, a strong black coffee and a cold shower to straighten up before she called Nick... After she did it all, she sat down on the sofa and dialed his number.

"Let me call you right back." And he put the phone down.

"Oh my God, I'm in deep shit," she said to herself. Her heart sank and her hands started shaking. She opened the window to let some fresh cold air in and started to breath deeply. "Calm down, relax. Nothing has happened. Not yet. He doesn't know anything. And even if he does, he will understand. Bullshit!!!

He'll understand what? That I'm a liar!"

She started walking around the apartment, like an animal, captured in a cage. Why hadn't he called back? Finally, her phone rang.

"Hi honey, sorry I couldn't talk to you, but I was in a meeting. How are you?" His voice was calm and soft and felt like a music from heaven to her. "I tried to call you before, but for sure you were sleeping."

"Aha" she said.

"So, do you feel better now? I felt so guilty, I had to rush out and leave like that today…hope you're not mad with me."

She thought she was dreaming. She could not believe her ears. A minute ago, she was breathing the fresh air, trying to calm down, fighting back the tears, panicking and thinking she'd lost him and now he was apologizing to her. The guilt started to eat away at her conscience. She sat silently on the sofa.

"Honey, are you still there? Please don't be mad with me. I love you." he said.

What was she supposed to say to him?

"I'm not mad with you darling. I've just been having a bad day." She really didn't know what to tell him.

"Did you get some rest?" he asked.

"Yes, I did, I woke up an hour ago. I'll be going to work in a while, so I wanted to call you to hear your voice, to say I'm sorry for being such a grumpy ass today. I really am. I love you babe."

She took a deep breath, praying to God he wouldn't notice that there was something going on with her. He could always tell by her voice if she'd drunk a lot or if she'd taken any gear.

"Are you sure you want to go to work tonight. Maybe, you should take a day off and rest." Nick suggested.

"Babe, I just came back from a month vacation and you're talking about a day off! I'm not tired. I only need to get used to the rhythm again and get used to not being next you all the time. That's all. I'm on it. By the end of the week I'll be in my old daily routine and everything will be fine. I promise."

"Ok, but if you feel like staying in, give me a call and I'll come to pick you up. We can watch a movie and order a pizza."

"I don't think it will happen tonight. I need to make some cash, but if all goes well, I'll take tomorrow off ," she added.

She'd made four thousand dollars already. She wasn't going to work on Wednesday. She finished her conversation with Nick and ran down to Andrew.

It was longer than half an hour since they left Joe's place. This was a stressful life, she thought. They parked the car in front of the building and Andrew left the key with the doorman in case it needed to be moved.

Joe, Jackie and Tom were still sitting on the table as she had left them, deeply involved in conversation. It was typical cocaine talk, where everyone is trying to save the world. She made a fresh drink for everybody, took a big, fat line and joined the group.

It was 6 am when she returned back home. She wasn't sure if it was still dark outside, or not. She wasn't sure about anything anymore. It had been a long, long night. She went to her room and fell straight asleep.

Chapter 35

Nick woke her up at 12 the next day.

"Good morning my angel!" he said.

"Good morning, my love!" Oh, was she happy today!

She had four thousand dollars in her drawer and no engagements for the day.

"I was dreaming about you," she said to Nick "It was a nice dream. We were on a beach and you were holding me in your arms. It looked like Hawaii."

"Is that where you want to go next, Hawaii?" he asked.

"No, into your arms. That's where I want to go, immediately!" she answered.

"I'm glad you are feeling better today. Go have a shower, drink your coffee, and oh, before I forget...I love you Mrs. Lucardi."

She smiled and put down the phone. Well, coffee wasn't a bad idea, but first she needed a couple of aspirin. She got out of bed.

The rest of the day went by with grocery shopping, a manicure, a pedicure and the bank. In the end she was almost late for 'General Hospital'.

Nick sent her a text.

"Pre General Hospital notice. Nicholas Walters is madly in love with Isabelle Lucardi." The world seemed to be in perfect order once again.

She took a nap after the show. It was late in the afternoon when he called her again.

"Are we on for dinner tonight, or are you going to work?" he asked.

"I miss my man so much, there is no way I'm staying away from him tonight." She sighed back.

"Ok. I'll pick you up at 8 o'clock from your place. I talked to my boss already, so I can leave earlier today, and I'll take you to 'Aureole'. It's on the Upper East Side. Supposed to be a real cool place, so get ready and put on something nice."

"What are you going to wear?" she asked.

"I won't have time to change. I'll come straight from the office…so, a black suit." Nick answered.

"I'll put something nice on for you!" Isabelle told him.

She took her time fixing herself up that night. She wore a nice suit from Versace. It was from last year, but she had worn it no more than twice. It was a salmon color knee length skirt and a tight blazer. It looked outstanding on her. She put on a pair of brown high heels from Gucci and picked out a matching purse. She looked million dollars!! She thought about taking one of her long cashmere coats, but then changed her mind at the last minute. They weren't going for a walk and Nick was picking her up from the front door. Instead, she picked a salmon-colored pashmina.

Nick turned up at 8 o'clock sharp.

The restaurant they went to was really classy. There were no more than fifteen tables. There was no music in the back ground and it seemed to Isabelle, that every table had its own waiter.

They took an aperitif at the bar, while their table was getting prepared. She looked around the room and studied the people in it. The men were all wearing suits and women were all very elegant.

She glanced at the man, standing next to her and squeezed his hand. He was looking so handsome and he was definitely the youngest one in the room. She felt so proud of him.

He might have read her mind, because he leaned towards her and whispered something in her ear.

"What did you say… I couldn't hear you." she said.

"I said, you are the most beautiful girl in the room, and I think we make a great couple."

They got escorted to their table. Nick ordered a bottle of Tignanello 97.

"I might not know how you drink your coffee, but I do know which one is your favorite wine." He kissed her gently on the cheek.

They ordered tuna tartar with beluga caviar to start and goose liver on a bed of rocket salad. As a main course Nick had the rack of lamb with a special herb crust and Isabelle, the venison.

"It's almost better than sex," she whispered "…and it lasts longer."

He gave her a strange look.

"I'm only joking, I'm sorry…actually, I'm not. I had the best culinary orgasm I've had for a long time." He had to laugh at her joke.

She wasn't joking though. Carlos, Isabelle's dad had been working in gastronomy for years. He'd raised her with an extremely sensitive taste for gourmet food. Carlos had managed five star hotels in Spain and Switzerland before he had moved to Mallorca. Isabelle shared her dad's passion for good wines and a fine kitchen.

For dessert, Nick ordered for himself a Crème Brulé and she asked for a cup of Fruit de Bois with a shot of Grand Marnier, which she poured over the top.

"I think, I am about to have another one…" She put her hand on his leg and laid her head on his arm, feigning delirium.

"Another one what?" he asked.

"Another culinary orgasm! "she replied, grinning.

The dinner was excellent, and she was in an exceptionally good mood. She was happy and she wanted to make him the happiest man in the world. She was in one of those giving moods. She wanted to give him everything she could. Please him in every possible way.

He paid the check, and she asked him to take them straight back home. She knew, in order to make her happy, he would've taken her to a bar, but she knew as well that he had to be up at 5.30 in the morning. So it was better to go back home and cuddle up. She wanted to show him all her love. She hoped he would never find out about the night before.

They drove through the streets of Manhattan, holding each other hands, smiling and she was sure, they were both thinking the same thing. How lucky were they to have each other. Things like this didn't happen every day. Some people never got to meet their other half and she believed that

Nick was her other half and she was his. Without him she felt incomplete. She looked at the stars and prayed to God.

"Please God, don't take him away from me. I know I'm not a perfect woman, but I'm ready to learn. I'll improve every day little by little and one day I will be the perfect one for him. One thing is sure, my love for him, knows no limit."

The next days went by quickly and before she knew it, it was Saturday. They spent the weekend nice and quietly, with no drugs or alcohol.

He took her to Soho on Saturday night and after dinner they went straight back home. On Sunday morning, she got up early and made breakfast. Scrambled eggs and bacon.

"I thought, you couldn't cook! Only spaghetti and salads," he joked with her.

"I'm learning," she replied.

Chapter 36

Frank came back to N.Y. on Sunday. He wanted to take her out for dinner, but again she found an excuse not to go. She knew she had to talk to him. It probably would be better if she moved out from his apartment and moved in with Nick. The next morning, she woke up early and went back to One Sutton Place.

Frank wasn't there, but she saw his bags in the living room. She picked up the phone and dialed his number.

"Hello stranger," Frank said, clearly recognizing Isabelle's number, "are you back in the apartment?"

"Yeah, I saw your bags, but you are missing," she said laughing.

"Are you going to be back soon…because I was thinking about inviting you for lunch?" she added.

"That'll be great. I'll be back around noon and I need to talk to you about something important, so lunch will be perfect." "What could be so important," she wondered.

Her cell phone rang. It was Charles Parrish. She'd been avoiding his phone calls for more than a month now. He wanted her to go with him and Grant Hamilton to another medical show in Fort Lauderdale in February, but she didn't want to be away from N.Y at the moment. Also, she still hadn't given him an answer about his job offer. She put the phone under the pillow to stop the ring tone from getting on her nerves. She made a promise to herself to call him later in the week. Her mind went back to Frank.

What could be so important, that he had to discuss it with her that urgently?

"Oh, my God, he's probably acquired that company in London and he's really going to set me up in London! But I can't see it happening. He never send me on any training and I still don't know anything about his business," she thought out loud.

She started to get nervous. What could it be? She didn't like surprises.

The coffee machine made a beeping noise, letting her know it was ready to serve. She made herself a cup and went to her room. She had barely been here since she'd been back from Europe. The cleaning lady had been there though, because all her laundry had been washed and folded and her bed had been changed too. She wondered why.

She started up her lap top and decided to kill some time by checking her emails and writing some back. She was surprised to find plenty of emails from Nick. He had sent lots of those silly singing greeting cards. Only his ones were really cute. There were a few mails from her sister and a few from some other friends of hers.

"I haven't heard from April for ages," she thought and decided to check up on her. She started typing.

"Hello babe, haven't heard from you for a while. Hope you are doing all right. How's London. I might come visit you for a few days on my way back from N.Y. I'm still with Nick and I'm still loved up. Ha ha. Write me back. Lol."

She pressed the send button. It was surely cheaper than calling. Not that it mattered, as she was using the land line to make international calls and Frank had told the bill gets paid by his company.

She missed April... her constant moaning and complaining, stressing everybody out around her. It sounded crazy, but she really was missing her.

Frank came back earlier as expected.

"Hello, hello! Let me have a look at you. You look like you've grown taller, little one, it's been that long since I last saw you.

What's it been?...month and a half now, or is it even longer?"

She was happy to see him again. Gave him a little kiss and stepped back, so he can have a better look at her.

"You look terrific. It must be the Spanish air or is it the mysterious boyfriend you've been hiding for long enough now." "Both!" she said. "How was your Disney cruise?" She followed him in the kitchen.

"Do you fancy a cup of coffee?" she asked him, "I've just made this. All super-duper fresh."

"Yes please. So, yeah we had great fun, you should check out one of those Disney cruises, but maybe wait a few years yet, they're more family orientated. The ship visits four islands in the Caribbean. They have beautiful restaurants on board and the best part is, they take care of the kids, throughout the whole day.

I saw my three boys for breakfast and then again at dinner!" He sat on the sofa and sipped his coffee.

"How was Spain? You flew back in last Sunday, right?" he enquired.

"No, I flew back from Spain last Thursday, but I was skiing in Canada until Monday. So, I've only been back here for a week."

"Canada, ah? Was it the mystery man who took you there? Did you go to Whistler?" he asked.

"No. Tremblant," she replied.

"So, who is he?" said Frank, fishing again for more info.

"I'll tell you at lunch," she rolled her eyes.

They finished their coffees and left.

"Where shall we go? You want to try Merchants or do you want to go back to Scalinatella?" he asked.

"Merchants is closer. I'm starving." Isabelle stated.

They walked down to the corner of the street. The weather was horrible. The streets were icy and there was so much snow on the sidewalk, it was hard to cover even a short distance. There had been two snow storms the week before and the city was having trouble cleaning up the streets. Numerous flights had been cancelled. She'd been surprised to hear from Frank last night, as she thought his flight would have been cancelled too.

"Where did you land yesterday?" she asked.

"Newark. La Guardia and J.F.Kenedy were closed because of the weather."

"I was wondering about that." she said.

They reached the restaurant and he opened the door for her. She took the green salad Niçoise with egg and tuna and he got the crab cakes.

"So what did you want to discuss with me? You said on the phone it was important."

"Yes. It's concerning the apartment," he started. "Remember I told you I was trying to move my office to N.Y.? Well, we are going to begin doing it from next month. My plan is to complete the whole transfer in two to three months. The thing is, I will have people from the office staying with me, every week…here in N.Y. So, the bottom line is I am going to need that second room."

She almost choked on her food. She was thinking about moving in with Nick, but not tomorrow!

"You said the beginning of next month…did you mean March or February?" she asked.

"February." came the reply.

"That's in two weeks. I'm not sure I can find a place to move out to, so quickly." Isabelle exclaimed in dismay.

"What about your boyfriend?" he suggested, hopefully.

By the timbre of his voice she could feel he was under pressure as well. She knew he wouldn't ask her to move, if it wasn't necessary…but it was still a shock for her. She had to tell Nick about it, but how? What was she supposed to tell him?

Frank wants me to move out and move in with you!"

"Hello, are you still there?" Frank interrupted her thoughts.

"Oh, yes. I'm sorry. I was just thinking. Well, I'll talk to him after this and let you know, but…I don't feel very comfortable asking him. I'm pretty sure he wants me to move in with him anyway, so if I give him a bit more time, he'll ask me himself." She fixed her eyes on his. "You know what I mean. If you could only wait till this coming weekend, then I can put the whole situation in a different light and it won't look like I'm desperate and have nowhere to live." Her eyes were begging him.

"Ok." He couldn't say no to her. "Do it the way you think would be the best for you. Just make sure you move out before the 5th of February. That will be in three weeks."

"Thank you darling. I really appreciate it."

"So, tell me now about this guy…what's his name?"

"Nicholas Walters. I met him in the club five months ago, but things started to get serious over the last two months. He came to stay with me in Mallorca for Christmas. We went skiing together in Tremblant. That's all." She was smiling again.

"How old is he?" Frank was not going to give up till he had all the details.

"He's 29 and he works as a broker," she said, knowing that would've been the next question.

"Why don't you invite him for dinner one day? I would love to meet him." Frank said.

"We can do that." Isabelle agreed.

They walked out of the restaurant and Isabelle reached for her cigarettes.

"I can't believe they won't let you smoke anywhere anymore in this city. Thank God, I can still smoke at work." Isabelle stated.

It was cold outside. Her fingers were frozen, so she threw the cigarette away. "Now I can't smoke outside either. What's wrong with this movie I am in right now?!"

Chapter 37

She didn't know exactly how to tell Nick about her new situation. Wait till the weekend and hope he will ask her himself, or tell it like it was? It was only Monday, so no need to panic…and she still had 3 weeks to go. She spoke with him a few times during the day, but never mentioned a word.

Monday was a slow night in the club usually, but not this Monday for her.

"Guess who's been looking for you?" Willow, the bartender, whispered from behind the bar when Isabelle passed by. "Joe Brown. He was here yesterday, but I told him you don't work Sundays, so he might turn up tonight."

"I hope so!" She got changed quickly and went back to the bar to gossip with Willow before it got too busy.

"Who was he with?" she asked.

"Who, Joe? As usual with that limo driver. They didn't stay long. Had one drink, asked about you and left."

She'd had her phone turned off last night. He'd probably tried to call her, but why hadn't he left a message? That was strange.

She hoped, he would come tonight. She finished her cosmo and went back to the dressing room. She dialed Joe's number only to hear the voice mail activated. Well, it was his turn tonight. Probably, they were out all Saturday and Sunday, so today he would be sleeping.

She went back to the bar and found Lashon talking to a nice looking guy.

"Jordan, come here please. Let me introduce you to Brien. Brien is from L.A, but he comes to N.Y. on business occasionally."

"It's a pleasure to meet you." He said turning to her and gave her a smile. "You very pretty lady!" "Thank you very much." she smiled back.

"Can I offer you a drink?" he asked.

"It's on the way" Lashon interrupted. She knew quite well Jordan would never say no to a cocktail.

Brien was an interesting man. He didn't reveal what was his business in the city but he seemed to know a lot about everything. No matter what the topic of conversation, he was always seemed well informed. They stayed at the bar for an hour, before they moved to the 'President club', a semiprivate room, more or less like a separate VIP lounge... The charges per hour were no different from those of a private room, so she knew her night was saved. Brien kept on ordering cocktails throughout the whole evening. He made her laugh a lot and she gave him a few dances. He was a very strange man though. It was hard to figure him out. Three hours later, she still didn't know any more about him than she had at the beginning of the evening. She didn't even get his last name, even though she'd asked him for it a few times. It was getting late. Brien decided to close his bill and go back to his hotel.

"Will you come back to my hotel?" he asked her straight out. "I'm staying at the Plaza."

"I beg your pardon? I don't even know your full name and I'm sorry darling, but I don't do escort services. That's why I'm here. If I wanted it to be different, I would have a website."

She was furious. How dare he? She hadn't done anything to make him think she would prostitute herself. Luckily the girls got paid up front for each hour of their time, so she didn't have to worry that he wouldn't pay her if she got mad with him.

"I'm sorry, I didn't mean to offend you. I was just thinking…" he muttered.

"I don't care what were you thinking. I can imagine what were you thinking. You thought that if I can take my top down for you, it isn't gonna bother me to take my bottoms off as well. Well, let me tell you it isn't gonna happen. So, dream on! By the way, our time is up and I have a friend coming to see me, so, if you'll excuse me, I'll walk you to the door." He didn't say a word.

"Have a good night, Brien." and she left him by the door.

After that little episode she went straight to the dressing room, got changed and went home. She called Nick when she was in her room. He was sleeping.

She was still steaming over that Brien incident and wanted to share her feelings with Nick about the whole thing but changed her mind at the last moment. "I'll tell him tomorrow, he is too sleepy now," she thought to herself. They talked for a short while and she then went to bed.

The next day she told him all about it.

"Can you imagine? I think he was fucking rude asking me that question," she said.

Nick was listening without saying a word. "Honey are you there? I can't hear you." "You are such a slut" he said.

She almost dropped the phone…

"What did you say?" she asked him, not believing her ears.

"I said you are such a slut. Did you enjoy flirting with him and teasing him? Did he touch you everywhere? How do I know you haven't given him your number and you'll not be meeting him today or tomorrow?"

She put the phone down. She had never heard him talking to her like that. Never! She had never even imagined him talking to her like that. The phone rang.

"Don't ever, ever again put the phone down on me." His voice was cold and threatening.

"What's your problem?" she asked "I haven't done nothing to deserve this. I told you exactly what happened and how upset I felt about it and you…what are you doing? Attacking me, as if I had asked him if I could go to see him in his hotel later. You should listen to yourself, Nick, calling me names. You know what, I don't want to put the phone down on you, but I do need to calm down, so I'll call you later. I need to think over what you said to me."

She waited for a second to see if he was going to say something, but there was only silence.

"Goodbye Nick." She put the phone down.

Chapter 38

She called Silvia.

"Hey sis, I need to talk to you."

She told her the shortened version of the story from the night before and described Nick's reaction and what he'd said to her.

"And he has never screamed or yelled at you before?" her sister asked. "Probably he's just jealous. Look, you're working in a strip club, it's normal that he'll freak out from time to time, but he still has no right to call you a 'slut'. If my husband called me a slut, I'd kick his butt right out onto the street in no time. Nick needs to apologize to you, and you need to stop telling him stories like these. Next time you call me first. I could use some entertainment!" They both laughed at that.

Silvia was right. She shouldn't have told Nick about Brien. Whatever, now she knew better for next time.

She went to take a shower. When she came out of the bathroom, there were six missed calls, all from Nick. She then checked her messages.

'Please call me back, I am sorry for what I said…' was the message from Nick.

That was fast, she thought, but decided to let him suffer for a while.

The front door opened and Frank walked in.

"Good morning…oh, I mean good afternoon. Did you sleep okay? I didn't hear you come in last night," he said.

"Good morning. I didn't hear you leaving this morning. Fancy some coffee?" she replied.

"No, I fancy something to eat. Do you want to join me for lunch? We can walk down to 3rd Avenue and I'll buy you a nice lunch at 'Scalinatella'." Frank offered.

"Mmm, yummy. What's the weather like outside?"

"Freezing! You'd better wrap up really well," he stated.

She grabbed a black cashmere scarf and put on a long cashmere coat.

"That'll do it," he said, "but don't forget your gloves. It's really cold outside."

He was 100% right, it really was freezing cold outside and it made her wish she was back in Spain right then, back in Mallorca, her beautiful paradise island.

She'd left her cell phone in the apartment on purpose. She knew that if she had it with her, and Nick called, she would have answered it, but she wanted to punish him, she wanted him to realize just how badly he'd hurt her feelings.

By the time they came back from lunch, there were sixteen missed calls. He'd sent her quite a few messages too.

'Please don't be mad with me.' 'I am so sorry.' 'I love you so much.' 'I freaked for no reason.'…and so on.

She smiled. It felt really nice, listening to his apologies. It felt as if somebody was pouring honey down her throat. She would give him another hour. Anyway it was 'General Hospital' time, her favorite daytime show on TV. He probably knew she was watching it, because he rang right after the show finished.

"Hi" she said.

"Hi. Are you still mad with me? I am sorry honey. I guess I got jealous when you told me about that guy. If I didn't love you so much, I wouldn't have reacted like that. Please forgive me." His voice was sad.

She could picture his face. His big eyes were probably not green as usual, but grey, covered with clouds of worries. She felt a little bit sorry for letting him suffer.

"I know you love me," she said, "but you have to learn to trust me. I trust you 100%. I would never even imagine that you would do something to hurt me. I would never think about you being unfaithful to me. So why do you think all those things about me? You need to trust me honey, because I love you with all my heart."

"I will. I promise you. I do trust you normally. I don't know how or why all that happened today. I guess I simply lost control of myself. It will never happen again, I promise. And I am sorry for calling you a 'slut'."

" What does 'slut' actually mean?" she asked him and they both laughed out loud. "I know it is a bad word, but I don't know the exact definition of it."

"Well, I'm not gonna tell you," he said and added hopefully "…so you're not mad anymore?"

"I'm alright. I'll call you before I go to work. Love you baby."

Even though she wasn't mad any more, a seed of fear and worry had been sown deep down in her heart. The way he had talked to her, she had never heard him so angry. What if it happens again! She tried to push the thought out of her head.

"I will deal with it, if and when it happens," she said to herself. The next morning Nick sent her flowers.

"They are beautiful," Frank said to her. "Are they from Nick?"

"Yes, we had an argument yesterday, and he's trying to be extra nice now, I guess," she answered and picked up the card attached to the bouquet.

'My love for you grows with every day.

I loved you from the beginning.

I love you now, and I always will!

Will you have dinner with me on Friday?'

That was very nice of him, she thought to herself and send him a message back 'Can't wait till Friday. Thank you for the roses'.

Frank was leaving that same day for Canada.

"We'll keep in touch," he said, "I'll be back in around ten days. So don't forget what I told you, I need this place all cleaned up by February 5th."

"Don't worry. I got it. You'll be late for your plane if you don't hurry up now."

She gave him his gloves.

"Call me if you have any problems. Okay?" he said.

"Frank, I'm not five years old. I know how to take care of myself. Let me know when you're going to be back."

"I am going to miss this flight if I don't go now!" He took his bag and ran to the elevator.

"All alone again," she said and closed the door.

It was Wednesday afternoon. She looked out of the window. It was snowing again. It reminded her of skiing… Tremblant, Nick…Nick, before he'd screamed and yelled at her.

"Oh God, I have to stop these bad thoughts. I'm not any better than him. Look what I've done too, I've lied to him so many times already! If he ever finds out about the night I said I was going to work and instead went partying with Joe…what's going to happen then?"

It was as if Nick had heard her she thought when her phone rang…

"I see you got the flowers," he said.

"Thank you so much honey. They are amazing…and so are you babe. Have I told you lately that I love you? I do, Mr. Walters… a lot."

"So where do you want to go on Friday my little princess?"

"To bed with you, my King!"

"That will be your reward , if you are a good girl throughout the evening and eat all your food", he joked with her. "Did Frank leave already?"

"Yes, ten minutes ago. I am all by my self and you know, I hate being alone."

"Why don´t you come over to my place after work. Then you won't be lonely any more," he teased.

So she stayed that night and all the rest of the week at Nick's place.

She would wake up around 11.30 am. He'd come home at 12 am with her latte. Sometimes they would make love, sometimes he would just hold her in his arms.

They went to 'Palm Steakhouse' on Friday and stayed in on Saturday. Sunday, they went to see a movie. It felt like they'd become a family. All the bad things were forgotten.

They went out for a drink with friends after the movie, then back home and made love again and again. She was melting from pleasure. He was making her world perfectly complete. Everything seemed to be great till Tuesday night the following week.

She was planning on moving in with Nick the coming weekend. They'd talked about it on Sunday before they'd gone to sleep.

"I wish you would be here all the time with me" he'd said. "I could make some space for your stuff in the closet."

She didn't say anything, but her heart started to beat faster.

"Just think about it," he'd said and stroked her hair, kissing her gently on her forehead.

It was all so perfect. It was all turning out the way she wanted it. She thought she was living in a dream...until Tuesday came...

...to be continued...

Is this a game or is it Love?

Sex, drugs and cash...or Love?

To find the answers to these questions, you need to step into Nick and Isabelle's mad world. Follow them through their journey of love, passion and sex, and along the way, their moments of utter happiness and deepest sadness. Their story takes them chasing each other around the world. They can't live without their love, but it's out of control and that journey will become a journey between heaven and hell.

A deliciously exciting love story that will make you laugh, cry, scream and dream again.

Welcome to New York, the Empire State.